THE POWER *of* TWO WEEKS FROM NOW

8/31/09

Dear Tim,

Thanks for the beautiful design on this book, inside and out. I love it!

In gratitude,

THE POWER

of

TWO WEEKS FROM NOW

HARNESSING THE POWER OF DENIAL TO MAKE YOUR LIFE SEEM BETTER THAN IT IS

Robert Crayhon

GENTEMAN PRESS

The Power of Two Weeks From Now
Robert Crayhon

Copyright © Robert Crayhon 2010

Genteman Press, Inc.
54 Madison Avenue
Red Bank, NJ 07701 USA

Cover and Interior design: Tim Jeffs

All rights reserved.
No part of this book may be reproduced or stored in any retrieval system in any form whatsoever without the prior permission of the publisher, except for brief quotes used in connection with reviews written specifically for inclusion in a magazine, newspaper, or website specializing in such reviews.

For information about permission to reproduce selections from this book, write to Genteman Press, Inc., 54 Madison Avenue, Red Bank, NJ 07701 USA

ISBN 13: 978-0-615-31089-3
ISBN 10:   0-615-31089-3

Library of Congress Control Number: 2009935243

Printed in the United States of America
10 9 8 7 6 5 4 3 2 1

This book is a work of fiction. Any references to historical events, real people, or real locales are used fictitiously. Other names, characters, places, and incidents are the products of the author's imagination, and any resemblance to actual persons, living or dead, is entirely coincidental.

A Note from the Publisher

On an afternoon in October of 2008, I was sitting in my office in New York reading London's *News of the World*. It detailed the escapades of the AIG insurance executives who were enjoying a lavish shooting party at a British country manor. While they cavorted about on their $86,000 partridge hunt and dined on pigeon breast and halibut, American taxpayers were bailing out their company. I marveled at their ability to ignore the realities of this world. I put the paper down and wondered, is there a way everyday people could engage in denial of this magnitude? Perhaps the inbred smugness of these higher-ups was beyond the average citizen, but was there a way regular folks could learn how to deny with such ease and on so vast a scale?

A manuscript then slid onto my desk. It was the book you now hold in your hands: *The Power of Two Weeks from Now*. I read it in just over two weeks, interestingly enough. I realized that I had just experienced one of the most transformative books of my life. Overall, I admire the broadness of its scope, the tenor of its argument, and the arrogance of its conclusions. Whatever it is saying, it is sure of itself, and that, these days, is rare. I became eager to know if the book would have the same effect on others as it had on me. It spoke to me in a way no other book had—especially when I was listening to the audio version of the book.

The Power of Two Weeks from Now was first published in Papua New Guinea in Tagalog, a language not spoken there. Because it could not be understood, it was instantly revered as a holy book. Its revelations were thought to be those of a great and mysterious god. Thus the phenomenon of its long and storied history began.

Since that time, *The Power of Two Weeks from Now* has been translated into twenty-six languages. We have only published it in English and Tagalog, however. We got a bit ahead of ourselves in the translating department, and we're actually kind of embarrassed about that.

In this one extraordinary book, yard worker, spiritual teacher, and stand-up comedian Robert Crayhon details how to harness the power of denial for ourselves on a regular basis. After reading this book, you'll forget things with ease, brush things under the mat with grace, and remove annoying facts

A NOTE FROM THE PUBLISHER

from your mind with aplomb. Realities that used to annoy you will be easily forgotten, and the result will be a life that seems happier, richer, and more rewarding than it is. And this, it seems, is the only kind of happiness we can ask for these days.

So, here we are. You're holding this book, you bought it, and you're stuck with it. Unless you're reading this in a bookstore, which I think isn't fair. Why? If one can read a few pages of a book before buying it, why can't one sit through the first few minutes of a movie before paying for it, or marry someone informally before making it final? Unless, of course, the marriage is only for two weeks, and then it can be annulled, which is commonly done these days. Thus *The Power of Two Weeks* reveals itself in our everyday lives.

ENOCH FILLMORE, *Publisher*

Contents

The Purpose of This Book 1
Beginnings 3
Note to the Reader 9
A Life Torn Apart 11
Back in the Club 21
Harry Lisbon 25
Antonio Robinio 37
Umberto Slidell 45
Charles Covetous 55
Repak Dopra 59
Fiona Brophonsky 67
Wendell Vance 75
Meeting Master Lohan 81
Master Lohan's Effect Upon My Work 93
We All Use Denial 97
Mindfulness 105
Your Questions and Answers 111
How Can You Heal a Broken Heart? 121
You Are Not Your Brain 125
What Is Meditation? 133
Religion in America 139
Losing the Moon 149

More Questions About *The Power Of Two Weeks From Now* 157

Solving the World's Problems with Denial 163

The Importance of Denying Global Warming 171

Our Ideas About the Past Are Based Solely on Memory 179

Even More Questions About *The Power Of Two Weeks From Now* 183

The Power Of Two Weeks From Now in Relationships 189

Questions and Answers About Relationships 201

Traveling with Master Lohan 207

Relieving Depression in America 229

Denial Cookies 237

You Are Not Your Possessions 239

How to Use Denial in Our Everyday Lives 243

Is Suffering Meaningful? 249

Other Areas Where We Need to Stay the Course with Denial 253

How to (Temporarily) Conquer Illness with Denial 261

Watching the Ballgame 265

Back in Town 271

The Purpose of This Book

The purpose of this book is to help you chill out. As my spiritual teacher Master Lohan said to me a million times, you don't have to do anything right now. You may think you do, but you don't. You don't have to be fully present. You don't have to better your relationships. You don't have to confront or work on your emotional pain. You don't have to exert any effort in any direction.

Best of all, you don't need to concern yourself with reality. That may be the best news of all. You can give up on all of this forever.

Beginnings

Call me Kincaid.

    I have very little use for the present moment and what is going on right now and I rarely think about it. But this was not always the case. There was a time when I was obsessed by the desire to be completely present. It consumed my every moment. I wanted to become enlightened. I wanted to be like the Buddha. To be the Buddha. I put every effort into making this happen.
    I was very stressed, meditating day and night. I did everything I could to be in the now. I became more and more obsessed the more I realized that I might never become enlightened, and never reach full awareness and full presence in the now. I felt life passing me by. As each moment passed,

I realized another moment had fallen into eternity without me being present in it. I would mourn that moment, and then move on to the next one only to realize I hadn't been present for that one either because I was busy mourning the last one. This cycle continued endlessly. I then became aware that there was an infinite number of moments within a given day, within a given hour, and I wasn't present for any of them. This only intensified my pain. Just think: an infinite number of moments in each day, and none of them lived in.

The more I experienced this, the more exhausted I became. My health worsened. I was losing sleep, harming my relationships, and even my lawn work was suffering. I could never stop continually thinking about what was going on right now and whether I was being fully present—whether I was really experiencing all that was going on around me: a beautiful day, the smile of a child, the smell of a freshly opened bag of mung bean sprouts. Was I truly experiencing these events, or were they passing me by as I was getting on to the next project or next event in my life? The downward spiral only continued.

Then, as I was sitting on a bench in New York's Central Park on a sunny spring afternoon, watching people play softball and parents push their children in strollers, I had an overwhelming realization. It was one that would change the course of my life forever.

I realized I no longer needed to be present. I could let the obsession go. I would give away all the spiritual books I had bought. I would do nothing. And I would take two weeks and wait. I would not try to become enlightened. I would finally listen to the instructions of Master Lohan, who said that I would never reach enlightenment anyway, and that I should stick to my specialty, yard work, and just enjoy myself.

I had finally listened to his teaching—unfortunately, long after he had gone.

Suddenly, an incredible feeling of peace came over me. For the first time in my life, I realized that I didn't have to do anything for two weeks. I didn't have to become enlightened, or be in the present moment. It was as if the load of the world had been taken off of me. And I remembered the words of Jesus: "Come to me, all ye who are heavy laden, and I will give you rest." But who had I come to? There was no one here. Just the parents, their children, and the New York City Parks Department workers, doing their usual excellent job which so few take time to appreciate. I was all alone. I was simply giving up. I was dropping the load of needing to be in the present moment from my shoulders once and for all.

I felt human again.

I then had the series of realizations that have become this book.

The Power of Two Weeks from Now came about because I realized in that instant that:

- I no longer need to be in the here and now.
- Many of the problems I have can just be ignored.
- Obligations of all kinds can be put off for fourteen days.

- Ignoring is in itself a kind of bliss, one we need to embrace completely.

I had fully embraced denial. It was the great spiritual awakening of my life.

By putting things off and not doing anything for two weeks, we allow ourselves a chance to simply be. And that is the ultimate goal—to be in the moment. When a spouse or significant other asks us to mow the lawn, what they are saying is, "I don't want you to be fully present right now, or focus on your true nature—I want the grass shorter." While we must accept the responsibilities of home ownership and personal relationships, it is more important at times simply to be. Thus, we must cultivate an irresponsibility to give us the mental space that we need. Irresponsibility and a greater distance between ourselves and reality, then, is the root of all enlightenment. It turns out that knowing what to deny is one of the greatest things we can learn. Embracing *The Power of Two Weeks from Now*, paradoxically, allows us to learn what is important. Not our lawn, or the demands of our spouse, but simply our need to exist.

Little did I know that embracing denial would completely change my life. I realized that I did not need to answer my phone every time it rang, even if it might be an important lawn job. I did not need to respond to every email as it came into my inbox. I did not need to talk to everyone who addressed me. This was especially true for Mr. Leland, my landlord, when he came by for the rent. I could ignore him. I could, in fact, ignore everyone and everything.

    As I sat on the park bench, the warm feeling deepened: a sense of relaxation, of calmness, and of peace. The world changed forever for me in that moment, and I began to experience a kind of stillness I did not think existed. It hit me like an ocean of space from another realm. This experience of the joy of denial would become the cornerstone of the teachings I would share throughout the country: how we can put things off indefinitely, and become happier as a result.

    I sat and enjoyed the day. I watched the gasoline-powered leaf blowers push leaves noisily up into the air. I watched parents berate their children, filling them with neuroses that would take years of therapy to reverse. I saw planes flying into LaGuardia Airport leaving toxic residues that all of us would breathe. At last, none of this bothered me. I felt free.

    By embracing denial, my identity had bloomed as well. I had become myself. I was no longer just a stand-up comedian or the most sought-after yard worker in my home state of New Jersey.

    I had become a spiritual teacher.

    Since then, I have been walking in a daze of joy. I have been asked to share this wisdom wherever I go—at church bazaars, garage sales, flea markets, hardware stores, and auto repair shops while waiting for my car to be fixed. This was the single realization that made me who I am today. My only goal is that through this book I can share my joy with you, and help you experience this kind of bliss for yourself.

Note to the Reader

Every so often you will see these two words appear in the text:

Two Weeks

When you see this, take two weeks to sit and think about nothing other than the thoughts that have just been expressed. Ideally, sit quietly in nature for these fourteen days. This will give these ideas the optimal environment in which to sink deeply into your consciousness and transform your life.

It also means it will take you a year to read this book. So buy it, don't take it out of the library.

A Life Torn Apart

All who are lost do not wander. –MASTER LOHAN

The journey to my great realization all began when my personal life fell apart. It started when Kelly, my girlfriend of two years, left me for no reason one Saturday night. It started innocently enough with a conversation we were having during our quiet celebration of her 29th birthday. She sat in my house eating the romantic candlelit dinner I had prepared for the two of us. She complimented me on the meal, said the sauce was excellent, and that I had put everything in the microwave for the exact right amount of time. Then, she put her fork down and asked,

"Do you love me, Kincaid?"

I thought for a moment, and wanted to give her an answer of complete honesty. I closed my eyes, put my hand over my heart, and took a deep breath, meditating for an answer. She knew my commitment to the truth was complete, and waited as I sat thinking. I then said, in an answer I had thought through with my last therapist, "Kelly, all my emotional energy goes completely in your direction, and there are no other avenues that my emotions are going in nor anything else which takes my attention away from you, emotionally and personally speaking."

She slammed her knife down on the table.

"You always say that, Kincaid. I know you and your therapist worked that out." She took a deep breath. "But do you love me?"

I looked at her intently. This was the woman I had lived with and shared my life with for twenty-four months now. She was always so understanding and fun to be around. Spending mornings together picking eggshells out of my omelettes. Walking home together when I ran out of gas because of the broken gas gauge in the hearse. Dodging Mr. Leland together in the attic when he came over to collect the rent. And she was so good at playing lookout for old Mr. Leland. She could practically smell him coming from a block away. She sometimes worried about him kicking us out, but I told her we were very valuable to him. There was no one else he could find who owed him six months back rent like I did. I looked up at the ceiling. I then looked down at the microwaved asparagus. It was getting cold. I thought and felt as deeply as I could.

"I like everything about you," I said. "If that isn't love, what is? I love your hair, your eyes—"

"I know you love all my parts, but what about me? Me, the person, the Kelly I'd be if I were old and gray—would you love me then?"

Whew. She was really pushing it. I thought about when I visited her at the aquarium where she works, and how after she gave me a tour of it, she said that fish never really marry.

"Remember at the aquarium, when we looked at all the fish together, and you said that what makes the fish happy is to have lots of other fish to be around? I mean—"

"I know, Kincaid, but do you love *me*?"

"Well," I said, thinking as hard as I could, "I think you're nice. I especially like the way you're friendly to people you don't know at parties, the way you say thank-you to everyone in stores, and the way you pet all the dogs in the neighborhood when we go walking. I think you're the nicest person I've ever met. I would completely trust you with a nuclear bomb, if I had one."

"You have a nuclear bomb?"

"No. But what I do have," pulling a piece of paper out of my pocket, "is a poem I wrote about you."

"A birthday poem? Really? I love it when you write poetry," she said, looking happier.

I unfolded it. It expressed the deepest feelings I felt about her. I stood up and began reading it:

I hope you don't become a Rastafarian,
And make your head all sticky and filled with glue.
I like your hair all normal and shiny like it is now,
And how it lies on your pillow when I wake up next to you.

She got all upset.

"I am not going to become a Rasta just because Cleo is! We just hang out together! She's just my friend!"

"Best friend!"

"So?"

"You two are like sisters."

"Maybe that's because I've known her since kindergarten."

"I know. Kelly, I worry that—"

She didn't listen. She mumbled something about wanting me to mention "love" in the poem, ran out of the room, and before I knew it, she was upstairs packing. I followed her and asked her where she was going. She said to Cleo's, where else. I said the poem was about what I was feeling about her in the deepest way, and that it could begin a dialogue about what we both were feeling and that we could then move into a deeper sense of real emotion. She just threw everything into her big pink suitcase, and told me things I had never heard before—that I didn't listen, was a soft male, lazy, self-absorbed, not spiritually growing, and that I really needed to work on myself if I ever wanted to be with an evolved woman like her. I just stood there and thought how beautiful she was, how wonderful her straight, shoulder-length blonde hair looked, how fiery her pale blue eyes were when she was upset, but I didn't say anything. She got in her car and left.

I looked at the dinner I had made and couldn't touch it. I wasn't hungry anymore. I walked over to the Jade Garden Restaurant on Broad Street for a different atmosphere in which to think, and drowned my sorrows in a Chinese buffet. When the meal was over, I stared at the fortune cookie. These messages had never spoken to me before, so I don't know why I expected it to be different this time. Nevertheless, I opened the cookie and read something I'll never forget:

YOU MAY DO SOMETHING LIFE-CHANGING NOW OR IN THE NEXT FEW YEARS. OR MAYBE NOT. WHO KNOWS.

It was amazing. It struck me like a bolt of lightning. It was exactly what I was thinking: now, or within the next few years, I might do something different. I always thought things could change. Here was confirmation. Wow. It was one of those jarring coincidences where you realize that even a fortune cookie can talk to you about your innermost thoughts and give you that push in the right direction.

I walked home and tried to figure out what had gone wrong with Kelly. Maybe she didn't like the retired Mercury hearse I drove. All my lawn equipment fit in the back so perfectly. Maybe she didn't like that it was so old it only played eight-tracks that I kept stacked in the coffin area in the back, and how the whole thing smelled of embalming fluid. She had to hold her head outside whenever we drove anywhere. I told her the benefit was that we could always put the headlights on and run any red lights and get the right of way, but she didn't see it that way. I loved it when I was late for a lawn job. It's a beautiful thing to run red lights with everyone's approval here in Red Bank. It's like being a member of suburban royalty. Or maybe she just didn't like me. There were so many reasons for her to leave. It was confusing. It hurt a lot.

I got home and tried to distract myself by reading her favorite book, *The Michelangelo Code*, the best-selling novel that says there is a secret buried in the paintings of the Sistine Chapel. The Code basically says that Christians need to eat only kosher food if they want to get into heaven. I looked at the diagrams in the back of the book, and still couldn't understand how they figured this out. I made a mental note to visit the Sistine Chapel and see if I could find the other hidden messages in the ceiling paintings.

I then started reading one of my favorite writers, Carl Sagan, and came across this curious passage:

> But the fact that some geniuses were laughed at does not imply that all who are laughed at are geniuses. They laughed at Columbus, they laughed at Fulton, they laughed at the Wright brothers. But they also laughed at Bozo the Clown.

But wasn't Bozo the Clown a genius? Maybe the greatest of them all?

I then picked up another one of Kelly's books, a guide to Greek mythology. I started reading about relationships, and why men and women break up. I read how the gods split humankind in two, into man and woman, so we would spend all our time chasing each other trying to become whole and not achieve anything that might rival the accomplishments of the gods. I didn't think it was a good approach. I thought most of the skyscrapers and bridges built by men were created just to impress women. The more I thought about it, the more I realized the whole plan had backfired. Then the doorbell rang.

It was Halloween. I got up and opened the front door, and saw three kids standing there with expectant expressions on their faces, holding out their bags of candy. One was dressed as a rabbi, one as a priest, and one as a farmer's daughter. I looked over to the table and saw that Kelly had left a bowl of candy there. She always made sure everything was prepared. Then I stopped. The meaning of Halloween had been drained from me. Maybe it was Kelly leaving, or something else I was unaware of. But something was gone from the day—I wondered deeply what Halloween was for and why we went through the motions each year when we didn't even know why we did it.

What was Halloween, truly? Wasn't it just a time when we put on costumes pretending to be different "persons" so that the world would give us candy? Wasn't this symbolic of how we lived our lives the rest of the year? Didn't we wake up each morning and go out into the world adopting a false personality we wore mostly for strangers so we could come home with something to eat? What about our true selves? Was no one ever interested in them? Why didn't anyone go out on Halloween—or any other day of the year—as who they truly are?

Three kids stared up at me holding their bags open. I saw this as an opportunity for all four of us to grow and realize something about ourselves. I told the kids that in order to get a big helping of candy they had to write an essay on the true meaning of Halloween. Why did we celebrate it? What was it about? The rabbi, the priest, and the farmer's daughter took pens and paper and began writing. Other kids showed up and joined in on our little project.

They all spent nearly an hour writing, and soon my house was filled with kids of all ages, all in their costumes, thinking, talking, and scribbling. The rabbi sat at the dining-room table and began interviewing the other kids, who were soon arguing with each other. A cowboy and a Native American also joined in on the discussion, the latter saying that this was a white man's holiday forced upon North American natives who didn't even like candy. Soon their parents came by, wondering where all their kids were and what was going on. I told them we were all searching for the real meaning of the holiday, and getting closer every minute.

Some of the kids came up with good ideas, such as sending the candy they didn't eat to poor kids elsewhere in the world. Others suggested that you should only be able to wear costumes you made yourself. Some said you should spend the day visiting your grandparents and making homemade candy with them. None of them, however, grasped the real meaning of the holiday. Perhaps it had been lost forever, and was beyond our modern materialistic consciousness now. It had become about the candy, and we just had to accept that.

After the kids left, I realized I needed help in my search for meaning beyond Halloween. If I was ever to get Kelly back, I had to learn why I was tongue-tied whenever she talked about love. I had to show her my true self, and find out which costume, if any, I was wearing, and then learn to take it off, at least once.

Maybe going back to where we met was the best place to begin. The Comic Strip Live.

Two Weeks

Back in the Club

Do not seek and you shall find. –Master Lohan

In the days that followed, I reminisced about how I met Kelly. It was her birthday two years ago. Halloween night. I was doing stand-up at the Comic Strip Live comedy club in New York. She had come with her friends and sat in the front row. She was dressed as a maid, and I made fun of her costume and told her she could clean up the joint after everyone left. It was a stupid joke, but she liked it. She and her friends were standing at the bar after the show and we met.

    I knew the last place she would go was the club, but I got the sense that if I went there and performed, it would bring us closer together. I realized half the time it didn't even matter to her what I said up there, just that I was doing it. When my act stumbled, she didn't care. I took the train in from New

Jersey, and luckily they had saved my place for me on Tuesdays. I started my set the same way I always did:

"I don't mind daylight savings time. I just hate having to get up at two in the morning to change all the clocks."

"A friend of mine who used to do nothing had a near-death experience a while ago. Since then, he has been reading a lot of books. It makes me wonder if there is a test to get into heaven."

"Not much happens in my life. It's pretty boring. Now and then I have a near-life experience."

"Ever since they told me the earth is spinning, I've been getting dizzy...."

"I met a 21-year-old girl in a bar last night. I looked over at her and said, 'Do you realize you're old enough to be my girlfriend?'"

"They say the War of 1812 could have been prevented with a phone call, if we had that kind of communication back then. What if we had Instant Messaging? The British would have sent us an IM that said, 'Will burn down White House LOL.'"

"Making love is like hanging a painting. It takes two people to do it, and one person is usually doing most of the work. The other person sits there and says, 'A little to the left, a little to the right, perfect.'"

"Native Americans name their children after the first thing they see after the child is born, such as Red Cloud. My father did the same with my little brother. His name is Buxom Nurse."

"My social life is like a virus. It's not alive, but it could come alive at any moment."

"Our town has a picture sign on the Main Street to point people toward the library. It's a picture of a head and a book in front of it. Why do they need a picture sign to get you to the library? If you can't read, what are you going to do at the library?"

"My girlfriend just filed a complaint against me for not stalking her."

"My family comes from a very strict religious sect. They don't believe in sex before marriage, or sex after marriage. They believe in working hard for all of this life and having sex in the next life."

"I like roller-coasters and love to sit in them…but only when they are not moving."

"I went to a nude beach last week. There was nothing on it—no people, no lifeguards, not a thing."

"My friend has a very small lawn. He bought a riding mower. I don't know why. All he has to do is turn it on and the lawn is done."

The audience reacted well to the set. I got some nice applause. But Kelly wasn't there. I stood backstage and bumped into the other comics who said they liked my set as they got ready to go on. I felt like I had wasted my time. Why? I guess I was just retracing my steps, trying to find another Kelly, but I knew it wouldn't work. As Master Lohan would say to me one day, "You can step in the same river twice, but it's not going to do much more than get your feet wet."

The next morning, I realized I couldn't hope to find another Kelly at the club or anywhere else. I wanted the original one back. I walked up Monmouth Street in Red Bank and picked up a copy of *Therapy Heroes* magazine at the newsstand. On the cover was the smiling face, gray hair, and soulful eyes of famed psychiatrist, author, and thoroughbred expert Harry Lisbon, Ph.D., of New York City. Only an hour's train ride away, I realized, was the best therapist in the country. Well, I thought, let's put comedy on hold, and give Harry Lisbon a chance to help me figure things out. I gave his office a call.

Two Weeks

Harry Lisbon

There are never enough I Love You's. –LENNY BRUCE

Harry Lisbon, Ph.D., was founder of the world famous *Center for Loving, Listening, and Healing for Men* on the Upper East Side of Manhattan. All of his ads and interviews said that love and heart-centered listening were the key to growth and becoming your true self. Harry said he put compassion and care into each new patient he worked with. He charged $400 for a forty-two-minute session. While I had to get extra yard jobs to pay for our weekly visits, I knew it would be worth it. With Kelly gone, I had time for the extra work. My focus was now placed one hundred percent on personal growth and becoming the kind of man she wanted me to be.

After one month of therapy, I found out there were only three things Harry Lisbon was interested in: a patient's childhood, prescribing medications, and the *Daily Racing Form*, the newspaper of horseracing. Each day after our session, he bolted off to one of the tracks to place his bets and then watch the ponies run. This is why he insisted all our sessions be paid for in cash.

During our sessions he read the *Daily Racing Form* while asking me to go over my childhood again. Harry said his mind operated on a level where he could only do two things at once, and if I asked him to do just one thing at a time, his brilliant intellect would shut down completely and he would not be able to help me.

In our fifth session, we ran over by three minutes, making it last a full forty-five minutes. It was the first time I thought that Harry Lisbon cared about me. The next week, however, he asked that we stop three minutes early and keep it at thirty-nine minutes to make up for the three minutes we went over the previous week. He said he had to run out to watch a horse he was a big fan of named Reuptake Inhibitor. This horse was running in the third race at Aqueduct, and if we stopped early, he could get there just in time to place his bet and watch the race.

Harry was constantly trying to put me on medication. In our sixth session, I walked in feeling sad about Kelly being gone. He diagnosed me with *Sadness Syndrome*, and prescribed a new drug called Melcholia that had just come out to treat it. I didn't fill the prescription. This was just as well, because the following week, I received a postcard from

Kelly saying she was down in Mexico with Cleo and having a wonderful time, and sent her love. Her love! She sent her love! Wow. She had never sent me her love before. I arrived at my next session happy, thinking she might come back soon. He saw how upbeat I was and diagnosed me with *Happiness Syndrome*. He said this was particularly dangerous, because *Happiness Syndrome* might lead to a manic state, which, if left untreated, could lead to a slightly excessive consumption of alcohol and food now and then. He wrote me a prescription for a new drug to counter *Happiness Syndrome* called Joliva.

That night, I saw an ad for Joliva on TV with zombielike suburbanites walking through a park:

> *Feeling happy? Not everyone is. And if your happiness is excessive, it may depress others. Be considerate. Take the edge off your sunny disposition with Joliva—the drug for people with Happiness Syndrome. It's good to be upbeat, but not "more than happy." That can be rude. Joliva. For those times when your happiness is out of control.*

I read up on it and found that one of Joliva's side effects was that it actually made a subset of the happy patients who took it even happier, which was the condition it was supposed to treat. That didn't make sense, so I didn't fill the prescription.

On the next visit, I told Harry I didn't understand what was wrong with *Happiness Syndrome*. He said that he could tell that the happiness I had was like that of most people: shallow and carefree, and without any real substance. He said I had no way of knowing whether Kelly would ever come back, and shouldn't bank on it. What we needed to do, he said, was try to pursue the profundity of misery for a few years and work through that. He said if it all worked out I would come out of that with a deeper joy in the end. That is, if I ever came out of the misery he helped stimulate and prolong, he said, which not everybody did. But he said it was worth a try.

The next week, I got another postcard from Kelly. She said that she and Cleo were going to be staying in Mexico for a few months studying with a shaman they had met. I thought of all the shortcomings Kelly said I had the night of the argument, and that week I meditated as much as I could, thinking it would make me a better person. When I saw Harry Lisbon for my next visit, I felt very relaxed. He asked me to describe my emotional state, and I said I really didn't have a mood. He got upset, threw down the *Daily Racing Form* and said, "How can you expect me to help you if you come in here without a mood? You look too calm. What have you been doing?"

I told him about the meditation, and he said I now had something called *Calmness Syndrome*. He said it could allow me to wallow in a kind of peaceful state that, if left untreated, could keep me from confronting all the pain and anger he knew was buried deep within me. I looked at the prescription he wrote me for *Calmness Syndrome*—the new mild stimulant drug Agitato—and realized maybe he was right. Maybe I needed to stimulate myself out of this boring state so I could find out what was down deep within me. He also said that if Agitato didn't work we could always look into more powerful stimulants or maybe electroshock therapy.

That night I saw an ad for Agitato on TV:

It's good to be calm, but if serenity is getting the best of you, talk to your doctor about Agitato. Agitato is the only proven treatment for Calmness Syndrome. Agitato will get you stirred up, dissatisfied, and productive in life once again. Within a matter of days, you'll be your old self, manically reaching for those things that make you briefly happy. Agitato. For when calmness makes you think things are fine the way they are.

I didn't fill the prescription. I didn't feel like being stimulated. The next week I asked Harry about the "loving listening" his healing center was named after. I told him I had come here hoping to find a compassionate ear for my problems so I could discover their real-life solutions. He said that he invested all his compassionate energy into finding the right prescription for me. He said there was no greater sign of love between a therapist and a patient than when the right drug was chosen. We agreed, however, that he would not write me any more prescriptions until we had completely discussed the one thing that did interest him about me: my childhood.

The only trauma I could think of during my childhood happened at age nine, when my father decided that my sister, mother, and I had to form a vaudeville act. My sister pointed out that vaudeville had vanished decades earlier, but Dad said she just wasn't showing the old vaudeville spirit when she said that. To him vaudeville was a kind of religion. He said vaudeville had the answers to every question you would ever have if you gave it everything you had. He forced us to learn endless jokes and comedy routines, and tap dance for hours a day. We were rescued only when I was able to tap dance an SOS signal in Morse code just as a social worker happened to be walking by the dance studio we practiced in every day after school. She intervened, and convinced my father to give up the family quest for show business.

Harry Lisbon said he couldn't find any real trauma in my past to work with, and I had to think deeper. I thought as hard as I could. I remembered when my mother was resentful at our having to pay for high-priced nursing care for our aged Uncle Edward out west for years on end. She ran this note with his photo above the obituary column, next to the ads called "Still in Our Hearts" placed by families mourning their loved ones who had passed on:

Dear Uncle Edward,
We know you're our relative,
That much is clear.
But we're all really wondering
Why you're still here.

    Family life was mostly happy. We played a board game called "I'm Not Sorry" where we all learned to blame each other for everything. We argued a lot, but lovingly. And the high point of the week was on Sundays when we played touch football with the family from across the street. Our family was made up of predominantly borderline personality disorder patients, while most of them were schizophrenic. We were offsides a lot, while they always refused to give the ball back after a turnover.

    Our family background was confusing. My mother was Jewish and my father was Catholic, so I didn't know whether to just not enjoy life or to feel guilty about what pleasure I did have. I didn't understand Christianity. How could Jesus be born on Christmas Day only to rise from the dead four months later? How could He do this year after year? What was Judaism all about? Why was guilt so important? No one was interested in answering these questions, so religion remained something abstract and unknowable.

    Dad usually had stressful jobs. The worst one was when he worked at a lock company coming up with combinations. My favorites of his were 35-7-30 and 25-12-25. On the days when he came up with those, he was happy. Then, after two years, he hit a wall. The numbers wouldn't come. He came up with combinations like 7-8-9, or 0-0-0. Nobody wanted them. Locks were returned with angry letters. My Dad was laughed at by the brawny men who made the locks. He quit in disgrace.

There were times when there wasn't enough food to go around. Once, when we were all very hungry, my parents sat my sister and me down and encouraged us to play a special game they had invented called "Catch a Moving Car." They said it was a really fun game, and all we needed to do was tag a fast moving car! They also said it was much easier to catch a car that was coming right at us versus one driving away, and that we should aim for those. We got knocked down a lot, but they were right: it was very enjoyable and brought my sister and me many happy memories.

Meanwhile, everyone pitched in to help with family finances. My Jewish grandmother started a Boy Scout Troop. She made guilt badges, and our troop went on shopping jamborees. We learned bargaining skills. Our troop motto was "Never Pay Retail." I became a Mensch Scout. We had one rich Jewish uncle, but he was kind of crazy. He took all his money and started a Jewish airline, one which stopped in every city any of your relatives lived in, whether you wanted to go there or not. Flights from New York to Los Angeles took three days instead of six hours. It went belly-up.

When I turned thirteen, my father walked into my room

one night, and we had "the talk."

"What talk?" Harry asked, leaning forward.

"You know," I said, "the talk every father and son have around that time about being a man."

"Oh, that talk," Harry said.

"Yes," I said.

I told him my father sat me down and told me that the most important component of manhood in America was denial—that we men did things we never talked about. We worked for big corporations that polluted and treated workers poorly, and looked the other way. We knowingly consumed infinitely more resources than other nations around the world, and didn't want to be reminded of it. We invaded countries for no reason but didn't want to be reminded of it. That was considered rude and poor form. Dad said all of this was important for the building of the American empire, and we shouldn't question it. He also said it was crucial that the men in our family deny their emotions and keep their feelings hidden, and that I should do the same. The most important thing, he said, is that when you become a man, you must learn how to use denial to keep everything buried so you can be happy. If I did that, everything else in my life would fall into place.

I finally understood how everything worked and what manhood in America was really about. Plus, I was touched that my father had taken the time to tell me how the world, and our family in particular, worked.

I then started telling Harry about phobias I had had in my teen years.

"Fear—excellent," he said. "About what?"

I told him I had spent much of my adolescence afraid that I would turn into Norman Mailer when I grew up. He smiled knowingly, and said that Mailer-related phobias were common in people of my generation, and that it was actually a good sign that I was concerned about such a possibility.

I then told him that in my senior year of high school, another life-changing event occurred. The yearbook came out. I picked it up and found out that I was voted Most Likely to Follow The Middle Way. Now, I knew a spiritual path lay ahead of me—I just did not know where it was or what it would entail. All I knew was that at age eighteen, I was already one of the best lawn workers in New Jersey, and that, come what may, I would always have steady work. We had no money for college, and my grades were not great, so I left home and began working the lawns of the Garden State.

In the end, I told Harry that the most frustrating thing about my childhood was that no one truly listened to me or cared about what I was feeling. I just kept putting all my frustrations into raking the yard. He put down the *Daily Racing Form* and said that what I had experienced was called *Not Being Listened To Syndrome*, and that there was a new drug for it called Empatha. He wrote me a prescription. Empatha apparently helped you relieve all the frustrations and pent-up emotions caused by years of being ignored.

That afternoon, I heard an ad for Empatha on the radio:

> *Is no one interested in your problems? Do loved ones interrupt you the minute you start talking? Has all this left you feeling blue? Then talk to your doctor about Empatha. Empatha is proven effective for Not Being Listened To Syndrome, and will give you that warm, fuzzy feeling that comes from having a caring friend sit and really hear what you have to say. Empatha. It will listen to you.*

I never filled the Empatha prescription. I still wanted a real person to listen to me and didn't think a drug could be that effective.

That was the last time I saw Harry Lisbon. Reuptake Inhibitor won big at Aqueduct the next day, and he won so much on the trifecta that he stopped seeing patients immediately. He sent out a mass mailing saying he was moving on to other things. I never found out what he thought about my childhood. I realized that if I wanted help, I needed to go somewhere else. I wanted to get motivated, not medicated. Only that kind of change would bring Kelly back to me.

I figured the best way to make myself into the man she

wanted me to be with was to sit at the feet of the greatest motivator and life coach in the world: Antonio Robinio. I worked as many lawn jobs as I could over the next few weeks, and came up with the three thousand dollars for his weekend seminar in Hawaii. Before I knew it, I was on the plane, heading in the direction of what I knew would be a better life.

Two Weeks

Antonio Robinio

Praised be delusion. –Jack Kerouac

Antonio's story was amazing. He had gone from being a pizza delivery boy running numbers in the Bronx to being one of the top motivational speakers worldwide. He once weighed 452 pounds, but now was down to a muscular 220 pounds on his six-foot-four-inch frame. He had CEOs, leaders from the artistic and political realms, and other important people from throughout the world seeking his advice on a daily basis. He had written four best-sellers, had a beautiful wife, three mansions, a yacht, and a microphone permanently embedded in front of his mouth recording everything he said in case anything profound slipped out accidentally.

Four hundred other attendees and myself listened to his life story as we stood next to the gently erupting Mount

Kilauea on Hawaii on the first day of his "Erupting with the Power of Your Own Volcanic Lava Within" seminar. After his first motivational speech was over, he had us do a range of exercises that he said would build our confidence. One of them involved taking turns standing on a tree stump with our backs to the group. One by one, we each fell backward hoping to be caught. We weren't. We each hit the ground and bruised our backs on the roots and rocks. This was Antonio's way of driving home the point that we are on our own in the world and should never have the illusion that there is anyone out there to catch us when we fall or help us achieve our goals.

He then walked our group close to the live, flowing lava so we could see its power. "This is what is inside all of you," he said. "Molten, transformative lava. Lava that can form new continents, new worlds." Antonio then put sticks, paper, and pieces of stale bread into the lava and we all watched them explode and burn up within seconds.

He then gave us the Three Rules of Lava:
1. Don't touch the lava.
2. Don't camp within ten feet of the lava.
3. This lava is inside all of you and has the power to transform your life and the world.

He said the third rule was the most important and could change our lives, but that the first two had to be observed whenever we were near the lava itself. Otherwise, we might not survive to enjoy the fruits of the third rule.

We then went back into a large seminar hall down by the ocean and reviewed Lava Logic. Antonio said that by following the logic of lava, we would all find freedom, success, and joy, just as effortlessly as the lava itself flowed from the center of the earth out toward the sea and melted and changed everything that it touched.

Many of the attendees complained that they had read Antonio's books and had tried to make lava-like changes in their own lives, but had found making these transitions hard, if not impossible. There were high school dropouts who wanted to become professors, lawyers who wanted to become rock stars, chefs who wanted to become clothing designers, and printers who wanted to become astronauts. They all looked up to Antonio, and asked him how to get there. Every participant said he or she had the determination and the fire of the lava, but still couldn't make a change. Antonio said that if we enrolled in his MIM Program—Mob Induced Motivation—we would all get there. He said nothing changed people's behavior and maximized their abilities like mobsters. He convinced us that there was no substitute for having two friends of his from the old neighborhood follow you around for a month, pushing you to achieve your goals, threatening you with bodily harm if necessary.

Like nearly everyone there, I paid the additional $3,000 for immediate enrollment—a seminar discount off the regular price of $7,500. We all left the seminar knowing our dreams were already closer to reality.

When I got home, I decided my goal would be to write a novel, something really romantic like the books Kelly loved to read. Maybe that would impress her. My Mob Motivators, Paul and Vinnie, were assigned to help me get a rough draft finished in one month. After three days, I had barely finished the first two chapters. A black sedan pulled up quietly in front of the house. A middle-aged man with a limp, a scarred face, and sunglasses got out, walked up to the front door, and rang the bell. I opened it and said hello. Paul introduced himself and welcomed me to the MIM program. He told me I was going to get a lot out of it.

"So, how's the book going?" he asked. Paul did the talking, I found out, and Vinnie usually waited and read in the backseat.

"Fine," I said. "Here are the first two chapters."

Paul looked down, and kicked a stone off the porch, annoyed. He looked over at Vinnie who had his window open and then back at me.

"Vinnie wanted to see the first four chapters by today." He stroked his day-old beard. "Two isn't gonna cut it."

"Sorry," I said.

As I looked in the car, I could see Vinnie flipping through pages of what was probably someone else's novel.

"It's not good to disappoint Vinnie," Paul continued. "He gets involved with characters, and doesn't like things to end after two chapters."

He leaned in closer.

"He starts to break things when he's disappointed. You wouldn't want him to get upset, would you?"

"No," I said. "I'll have the next two chapters by this time tomorrow."

"That's better," Paul said, gently slapping my cheek, and then turning around to leave.

They came back the next day, and I handed Paul the next two chapters. Paul looked around like I was supposed to read his mind. He had yesterday's work rolled up and was patting his hand with it.

"What?" I said.

"Vinnie says the characterization is weak. Vinnie don't like weak characterization. This should go without saying. Also, he don't like that his favorite character has already died off. That really upset him. He cried."

"Sorry," I said.

"Don't make Vinnie cry that early on, kid," he said.

"All right."

"Vinnie suggests that if you want to live, you'll let the character live, okay?"

"Sure."

"Good boy," Paul said, patting my cheek once more. "Now, go inside and type more romantic stuff. And no more killing off nice people. And one more thing."

"Yeah?"

"I don't want to drive by later tonight and see that

television on, know what I mean? If you're a writer, you write. TV is for people who only dream about being writers."

"OK," I said.

He got back in the black sedan and they drove off.

A few days later, the day was so beautiful that I decided to take the afternoon off, and went to an outdoor café in Sea Bright to take in the brilliant sunshine and relaxing sea air. The sky was blue and the wind was snapping off the Atlantic while I enjoyed my hot chocolate. As I sat watching people walk by, a black sedan pulled up in front of me and slowed down. Vinnie rolled down his window and lowered his sunglasses slightly as he glanced in my direction.

"So, you done?" Vinnie said.

"No," I said.

"So, whatcha doin' here?" he asked.

The window then went up and the car took off. I went home and got back to work right away.

At the end of the month, I finished the rough draft, and Vinnie said he liked it so much there was no reason for me to end up with any broken bones. I heard from other people in the program that if your Mob Motivators didn't break anything, chances were that you had written something decent, maybe even good enough to be published.

The next week, I wrote an even better ending, and got really excited about what Paul and Vinnie would say. But Paul and Vinnie were no longer coming around in their black sedan. I knew the month had ended, but I still wondered why they didn't show up. I started feeling lonely. I missed those guys. Sure, they threatened me, but they cared. Somebody doesn't say they're going to break your index finger over a bad description of a sunrise unless they're really interested in your writing. Nobody had been as invested in my work as those two. I called up Antonio Robinio's office in Marina Del Rey, California, and asked if Paul and Vinnie might be coming around in their off-hours. They said no. They said that if I wanted any more threats coming my way, I was going to have to pay for them upfront and without a seminar discount this time. I was out of money, so as far as motivation went, I was on my own. I decided to set the novel aside until I could get motivated about it again.

To clear my mind of Antonio Robinio and Paul and Vinnie, I finally sat down and watched the entire *Police Academy* DVD box set Kelly had gotten me for my birthday. It was the perfect gift. I realized after watching all seven movies in a row that only when you see them back to back do you get the whole gestalt of what the creators were going after in this series.

It was midnight, and I felt I had learned nothing from Antonio Robinio. I looked into the refrigerator and Kelly's birthday cake was still sitting there. I had put trick candles on it for her, the kind that keep lighting up after you blow them out. I lit them again, and tried blowing them out, and watched them light up again each time. I realized that was how I felt about Kelly—I kept trying to blow her out with my mind, but in my heart she kept coming back and

lighting up again on her own. Candles you can't blow out.
It was getting late. I started flipping the channels. As I got to the religious stations, I saw all the preachers. I began to think about the kind, devout, hardworking, and violent Christian brothers who had taught me so much about God and the moral improvement brought about by physical pain when I was a teenager. I closed my eyes and fell on my knees, praying to God that He would show me a way to improve myself to the point that it would bring Kelly back. In a miracle of sorts, my prayers were answered immediately. I looked up through my tear-filled eyes and saw the most famous Christian evangelist in America—the charismatic and compassionate Pastor Umberto Slidell—preaching right at me.

Two Weeks

Umberto Slidell

An unhurried sense of time is in itself a form of wealth.
—Bonnie Friedman

Umberto Slidell preached nightly from his World Evangelical Outreach Headquarters in Houston, Texas. After watching him that night, I bought his best-seller, *Get All the Stuff God Has Coming to You*. It was an inspiring read. Heaven wasn't some far-off concept to Pastor Slidell—it was in the here and now and consisted of material possessions. God was in the business of making sure we had everything we wanted, as long as we asked for it in prayer while obeying His word. Car dealership lots were filled with cars, Umberto said, because we were all supposed to have one. Otherwise, why would they all be sitting there? It was only our lack of faith that kept us from having these and all the other things we wanted and indeed deserved.

Umberto grew up in Alabama, and received a "special

anointing" while playing Monopoly with his sister when he was eight. According to his father, he suddenly got up after landing on Boardwalk, and walked around the house holding the deed, staring at it, and looking at the high rents he could charge his little sister. Umberto then put down the deed and immediately started reading the Bible, saying that heaven had the most valuable real estate, and that he had this vision of all the people of America coming together and giving him money. His family traces his ministry to that day.

Umberto went to college and then on to seminary. He showed early talent as a preacher even while in school, and helped out at revival meetings all over the South. Yet while Umberto was a Protestant, he said the Protestant Reformation had gone too far. Selling indulgences wasn't that bad an idea, he said to one of his professors, because it helped pay the bills and kept the followers in line. That statement got him kicked out of seminary, but Umberto's skills were so great that his followers didn't care if he had a degree. The spirit of God was running through him.

This sermon, which I heard the second time I saw him on TV, was the one that made me believe he could help me change my life:

> God has said that if we just had faith the size of a mustard seed, we could turn that seed into a mountain. Now, your checking account is nothin' but a mustard seed—a pitiful, embarrassingly small

amount of money. It disgusts me to even think about it. Maybe you only got fifty dollars in it. And you've got bills piled high and children cryin' 'cause they're hungry. If you would but have the faith of that mustard seed, and let that seed die—send whatever you can to the address on your screen—you would let that seed fall into the rich, moist soil of God's anointing where it can sprout, take root, and grow to spread the Gospel of truth around the world.

Now, I have two indoor basketball courts at my house. Two! And to think I grew up suffering in middle-class suburbia where we drove only used cars and wore mostly hand-me-downs throughout my childhood. Both my parents worked. No fresh-baked snacks for us children—only store-bought cookies when we got home. And look at me now! I can play basketball at three in the morning if I want! This is what faith can bring! You have to let go of something to keep it—so let it go, let that mustard seed of a checking account find its way to us here in Houston, and we will pray for you and send you our precious Wealth Prayer Shawl. You can wear this shawl that we have prayed over when you go job searching. You can wear it when there isn't enough food on the table and everyone is hungry. Many believers have told us it suppresses their hunger pangs. You can wear it when the bank forecloses on your home, when the bills pile high, and when your children are moaning with hunger. You will feel the power of God coming through you no matter what may be happening! Remember that God is greater than any problem you have. So let it go—let go of all that money so He can fill you with His riches. You have to make room for God's blessings. You have to create a new wineskin for the new wine. Make room in your life, and send your money in now.

I was amazed. How did he know I only had fifty dollars left? I sent it in right away. The next week I got my Wealth Prayer Shawl in the mail, and watched to see if my checking account would grow. That Friday, as if by divine intervention, sixty-two cents of interest accrued in my account. I was beginning to see faith bring miracles into reality.

The next Saturday, Pastor Slidell told us the story of the day he knew he was going to be a successful preacher:

When Lynn and I started out with our three little ones, I remember the Saturday when we had a birthday party for our youngest, Daniel. He had just turned five. We had a party for him and all his little friends in the backyard of our small house in Little Rock. We had a cookout, and Daniel asked me if there were any more hot dog buns, because his was broken. I looked in the package and we were out. I said no.

So, little Danny sat there eating his hot dog in a broken bun, with tears streaming down his face. I vowed right then and there that our family would trust God, and that we would never have to serve our children broken hot dog buns again. We have never looked back, and have trusted God for all the abundance and riches we enjoy today.

The idea of a small boy eating a hot dog with a broken bun shook me up. That sort of thing should just not happen in America. I was glad that Daniel was rescued from ever having to face that fate again, and cheered along with the crowd in Houston at the triumphant end to the story.

The next week, Pastor Slidell opened his heart and wept right into the cameras as he began a major fundraising drive to help the poor in his area:

> You see here on our stage eleven gleaming white Rolls Royces, polished to a shining luster to mimic the perfect power and justice of God. Our deacons spend hours every day before the service polishing these cars so they mimic the untouchable purity of God's perfection. And every Sunday after services, we drive them through the poor neighborhoods here in Houston. I can't tell you the blessings people receive when they come out of their broken-down homes in their ragged clothes and see the glory and power of

God reflected in these sanctified vehicles. And yet, what could be more pitiful than having eleven cars when God had twelve disciples? How can we shortchange God? That's where you come in. You are able to deliver a profound message to the poor by helping us get the twelfth charity vehicle. For what God has begun, He will finish with our help. He has told us He will abandon all the other lambs to get the one that is missing! Help us reclaim that missing Rolls Royce! The blessing that the poor shall receive when they see our twelfth car turning the corner into their neighborhoods—neighborhoods where the police and fire trucks dare not go, mind you—will make them cry out to God in joy! They will fall down on their knees and praise the Lord, and see His glory reflected in the chrome wheel covers and polished wood-grain interiors of our holy entourage. They, too, will see that wealth can come to those who seek it, that a man who grew up eating store-bought cookies can now taste God's blessings in abundance. They will be inspired not to give up on life. We have letters testifying that our Sunday pilgrimages have kept families together. And as soon as we have the twelfth charity vehicle, one for each disciple, one for each of the twelve tribes of Israel, blessings of an unimaginable nature will shower upon us all. But you must take part in giving those blessings in order to receive God's gifts in return. We must only ask of God, as I am doing now of you, and He shall give us all that we need, just as you have given me all that I need. Let us always be in accord with His will, and only then can each of us have all of the things we truly deserve.

Over the next few weeks, the poor people of Texas sent in five and ten dollars each, and Pastor Slidell got his twelfth Rolls Royce. I watched him on TV as he drove through the poor neighborhoods of Houston with his procession. People cried out and fainted, calling out to God in joy with their wishes for wealth. It made the cover of national Christian magazines.

But I had begun to lose interest in Umberto. He didn't seem anything like the Christian brothers who had taught me in high school, who had lived a humble and dedicated life, and spent their lives just trying to keep their school alive. On top of that, my Wealth Prayer Shawl wasn't doing its job. I had nothing left after sending in whatever I had to help Umberto get that twelfth Rolls Royce.

Another crisis soon hit Umberto's ministry. He said he needed to raise twenty million dollars to stay on the air with his nationwide broadcasts, and called on his faithful supporters for help. He said that if he did not receive the money in two weeks, God would call him home. Some of his supporters asked him if it wouldn't be better to be in heaven than on earth, as the Bible said. This caused Umberto to excommunicate those followers. I stopped watching his sermons after that.

The more I thought about Umberto, the more I wanted to reconnect with the original words of Jesus. I no longer liked Umberto, but from my days with the Christian brothers, I had developed a real love for Jesus that never vanished. My head started to crack trying to figure out how I could lose interest in the most famous preacher in the country but still love God. To calm myself, I turned to the Sermon on the Mount:

Blessed are the poor in spirit
For theirs is the kingdom of heaven.
Blessed are those who mourn
For they shall be comforted.
Blessed are the meek
For they shall inherit the earth.
Blessed are those who hunger and thirst for righteousness
For they shall be filled.
Blessed are the merciful
For they shall obtain mercy.
Blessed are the pure in heart
For they shall see God.
Blessed are the peacemakers
For they shall be called sons of God.
Blessed are those who are persecuted for righteousness' sake
For theirs is the kingdom of heaven.

I thought, why couldn't they just throw out the rest of the Bible and keep this part? It's the best part. But it probably wouldn't make a lot of people happy, especially Umberto. It doesn't go along with anything he says. I bet he would take it out of the Bible if he could.

The next day, I got a postcard from Kelly. She was doing great. She said she and Cleo were still in Mexico studying with the shaman and everything was going really well. She said they had also gone whale watching and had a great time. The same day I got a flyer announcing that the Mormon Tabernacle Choir was coming to Carnegie Hall with an all Fats Waller program. Kelly would love it. I could see her smiling and swaying to their rendition of "Fat and Greasy," her favorite song. I wished we could go to that concert together. I dreamed of her flying up just for that weekend. The more I imagined it, the more puzzled I became about why things hadn't worked out with us.

I realized the first thing I needed to do was to become more successful so I could at least afford to fly her back for things like this. Even working double-time on lawn work wasn't enough. Maybe the best way to increase my income would be to become a successful businessman and start a nationwide franchise of lawn workers: Reliable Rakers. I saw that Charles Covetous was coming to town, the man who had helped thousands to create their own businesses and rise to the top of the corporate world. Maybe he could teach me how to put a plan like this together. I signed up for his seminar right away.

Charles Covetous

Why be a man when you can be a success?
—BERTOLT BRECHT

The legendary **Charles Covetous** displayed a powerful ability to make money from a young age. In the fifth grade, in his hometown of Elyria, Ohio, he started a corporation, sold stock to his classmates, and then declared the company bankrupt. He kept all the money, and used it to fund his first teaching organization. By eighth grade, he was already holding after-school courses for fifth graders on how to swindle fellow students out of their lunch money so they could begin their own corporations. He was on his way.

In preparation for spending a weekend with someone *Time* magazine called "the man who made more money off seminars than anyone else," I read his best-selling guide to the successful life, *Six Principles for Being Extremely Effective in*

All Areas of Your Life. Here are Charles Covetous's six principles for guaranteed success:

1. Don't make any mistakes.
2. Compliment your coworkers and bosses as often as you can. This way, you'll have friends to help you cover things up when you do make a mistake.
3. Do the things you want others to see you do.
4. Don't get caught doing the things you wouldn't want to be seen doing.
5. Work smart. Copying something by hand shows your solid work ethic, but is not as efficient as using the copier. Learn how to use all the office equipment during your first week at work.
6. Don't assume you know what you don't know. You might not.

The seminar was bracing. We all learned lessons we could instantly apply in the business world, such as time management strategies. For example, instead of watching soap operas all day, he suggested we read *Soap Opera Digest* instead. Or, if possible, have an assistant watch them and leave an executive summary of them on your desk the following morning.

We broke into groups and played out various business scenarios. In the first one, we each did things we knew needed doing but that others wouldn't do in the office. These included replacing the water bottle at the cooler, or putting more paper into the printer. We role-played and saw how we could make these things happen more efficiently. It was fun. Next, we all took turns pretending to ask someone how the office equipment worked. Finally, we all went around complimenting everyone and tried to turn them into our office allies.

The next day, we wrote a list of the ten most important things we wanted to do in life. Then, he told us to look carefully at that list and rewrite it in the order of greatest importance. We reorganized our lists. I now looked at mine, which had somehow transformed itself into what I knew I wanted to do with my life, and in the order I wanted to do it. It was magical. I could already feel my life shifting in the right direction.

At the end, Charles Covetous spent two hours drawing a complex diagram on the board from memory. After he was done, he had put everything that helps you get ahead and increase your effectiveness in life inside the big circle. Everything that didn't help you was outside. He then said, "Now, just throw away everything outside the circle, and you will be a success in life." We were amazed that it was that simple. We gave him a standing ovation.

Despite the high of my newfound success plan, I left the seminar feeling empty. I walked into an Italian restaurant to collect my thoughts. When the waiter brought the bread, I took a piece out of the basket, and just as I was about to eat it, I looked at it and realized it was in the exact shape of the head from the famous painting, "The Scream." It made me realize I wanted to scream. I hadn't learned anything I could use from Charles Covetous. Nothing I had learned would help me start Reliable Rakers. Sure, I would try not to make any mistakes, and be certain to ask how all office equipment worked should I ever get a desk job again, but past that there wasn't anything I really felt more effective at. Complimenting the waiters didn't make the food come any faster or taste any better. Plus, they made mistakes, but did not lose their jobs. I knew Kelly would not come back just because I could avoid mistakes, compliment coworkers, or operate a fax machine. She wasn't looking for me to be more effective at anything, in fact.

Two Weeks

Repak Dopra

You grow older only by thinking the wrong thoughts.
—Repak Dopra

That week, I was busy with more lawn work than I could handle. In my spare time, I read and reread Repak Dopra's best-selling book, *Imagining Growing Younger While Giving Me Cash*. Its main idea was amazing. By using the principles of quantum physics to alter the way our perceptions dictate the reality we lived in, we could slow, if not reverse, the aging process. This was probably the greatest discovery ever made. Repak wrote:

> The molecules in the universe that we now see are in their constituent parts invisible. Yet when they come together, the protons, neutrons, and electrons suddenly enter the visible spectrum. This is how the aging process works. You can't see it, but it's there.

As simple and direct as his writing was, I couldn't understand it. I realized I needed to take his seminar in order to incorporate all this into my life. As I walked into Madison Square Garden that Saturday, I couldn't wait to learn more about what Repak had discussed in his book. Men, women, and children from all over the world had come to have their diseases cured and to witness as Repak told us how to join his health revolution. All ten thousand of us wanted to stop the aging process and heal our bodies. At 9:00 a.m., he hobbled out onto the stage with a cane and began by telling us how the aging process could be stopped once and for all:

> The universe creates infinite intelligence inside every cell, which creates everything around us. Each cell uses only a small amount of its intelligence, and yet we can still create symphonies. Conquering aging is no different. We merely must put our minds to it, and like the music that wafts over us in a concert hall, the process of aging can stop.

We felt as though the aging process itself was slowing down and even reversing as he talked to us in his hypnotic and soothing voice. Repak continued:

> If you have a disease, it is only because of negative concepts that are taking up residence inside your

mind. By eliminating negativity from your consciousness, you eradicate disease. Except for limbs that are broken. Those will need a cast. Cancer, however, is a state of mind. If you are open to healing, it will manifest in your body. If you die of cancer, it is your fault. You have not rid your mind of enough negativity.

A huge sigh went over the hall. It was as if we had known this deep down all along and it was finally being revealed to our conscious selves. I saw a lot of guilty faces all around as people realized they had caused their own diseases by holding on to bad emotions.

Repak then answered questions about specific health problems. I walked up to the microphone and asked him about my high cholesterol. He said:

If you have high cholesterol, it is because too many calories have entered the space-time continuum with elements formed in the furnace of supernovas billions of light years away in ages long gone. These molecules have now manifested inside your arteries as a variety of fat globules. If you are eating too many of these supernova fragments, especially those found in pork rinds, try cutting back. Also increase exercise.

It was almost exactly what my doctor had told me, except

all he said was to cut back on the pork rinds.

On Sunday afternoon, Repak told us he was about to let us in on the most powerful antiaging secret the world had ever known. He said we would now be special initiates into his inner knowledge. This was the secret that had been handed down to him from masters he had studied with in India, Tibet, Bhutan, and Cleveland. The entire group knew this would be the high point of the seminar. The lights dimmed, and ceremonial music wafted through the loudspeakers. Repak brought in a large, ornately painted tureen which we could see up close on the monitors. Repak moved his hands over the tureen in what looked like an ancient rite. He then removed the lid to reveal a medley of cooked vegetables. Repak then told us to vow to ourselves that we would eat a variety of vegetables every day, ideally, five or more servings. The more of them we ate, he said, the less we would see aging manifest itself in our bodies. We all chanted about vegetables for the next three hours, especially broccoli and brussels sprouts. We then walked out onto Seventh Avenue in a reverie. We each knew our lives had been changed forever.

The one thing I could not understand about Repak was why he looked so old. He appeared at least thirty years older than the photos on the cover of his books, which were themselves only five or ten years old. He was overweight, looked tired, and needed to sit down often to catch his breath if he spoke for more than a few minutes. He explained that his accelerated aging came about because he had used so much of his karmic energy to help others liberate their negative emotions. Looking at the bags under his eyes and his large stomach, I could only sympathize with him for taking on the world's suffering. I realized Repak was, like all great spiritual teachers, a selfless and giving man who asked for nothing in return, and who had given up his health as a result. It was that message of sacrifice more than anything else that I took away from the weekend, although I also bought four of his books and five of his CDs, as well as a subscription to his monthly newsletter.

When I arrived home, I put one of Repak's CDs in the stereo right away, the one on driving meditation. This one interested me greatly, because Kelly always said I was a distracted driver. Maybe this CD would help me become more focused behind the wheel. Since the only thing in the hearse was the eight-track player, I would only be able to listen to it in the house. I put it on and lay down on the couch, ready to learn how to become a more focused and meditative driver:

> Now that you are driving, close your eyes. Trust the control of your vehicle to your other senses. You have driven this vehicle many times before. You do not need visual confirmation of what you are doing. Trust your hands. Trust the sensations coming through your feet. Connect to the way the roaring motor feels throughout your body. Let intuition guide you. See if

you cannot feel the sides of the road, the pedestrians, and the other cars with this newfound inner confidence.

Perhaps people are yelling at you to drive more in the center of your lane. Let them shout as you remain in your quiet state, in the center of your being, letting your inner senses drive. Ignore their attempts to bring you down to their mundane level of consciousness. Perhaps they are screaming at you to avoid something. Don't let this distract you from your inner journey.

You may now feel a jolt, and the sounds of metal smashing and glass breaking as you feel yourself being jostled in your vehicle. Don't let this pull you out of your relaxed state. Keep both eyes closed. Stay calm. Perhaps an airbag has exploded in your face. Feel its soothing contours support you like a meditation pillow.

The smell of gasoline may now stimulate your nostrils. Feel how much more pungent it smells with your eyes closed. Send deep gratitude to this magical distillation of dinosaurs that has selflessly propelled you through many years of happy driving. Breathe deeply.

You may hear people right next to you now, urging you to vacate the vehicle. Keep listening to my voice. Perhaps in the distance you also hear the sirens of emergency vehicles drawing closer and louder every moment. Let everything happen without your involvement. You are an example of peace and perfect detachment from what is going on around you. You are bringing joy and enlightenment to the world. You are a model of serenity and concentration for all to remember.

I got up off the couch and turned the CD off. I had a hunch there was something wrong with this approach to driving, but I wasn't sure what. Though I felt more relaxed, I realized that all this relaxation was not the key to solving anything—I would just sleepwalk through life, whether in a car or on foot. What I needed to do was wake up and solve the problems I was facing with Kelly. I needed to be more alert and focused, not just serenely accepting everything around me.

Two Weeks

Fiona Brophonsky

Association with human beings lures one into self-observation. –Franz Kafka

That week, while supervising a hedge-planting job in Rumson, I suddenly realized why things had not worked out with Kelly and me. It wasn't because my hands were often covered with calluses from raking or working outside. It was that we had needed a relationship expert to help us but never had one. Maybe we should have gone to couples therapy. We had not followed any set rules—we had just dated, gotten to know each other, had a wonderful time, and then after six months had begun living together. There was no structure to it, and that may have been the problem. Aren't structure and commitment what everyone needs? Maybe I could read up and find someone to help us with this in case she ever returned one day.

And who better to teach relationship structure to me than the pudgy, aggressive, whining, yet charismatic Fiona Brophonsky, queen of public television relationship seminars, and author of *The Fourteen Relationship Rules: Live By Them or Die Alone*. Her one-day seminar promised both men and women that they could learn how to get the mates they wanted and keep them happy forever. With a promise like that, I signed up right away.

When I arrived at the midtown hotel for the seminar, we were all given large binders that contained all the material we had to work through that day. The focus of our work was the fourteen rules, which she said helped countless awkward single people find their mates:

RULES FOR WOMEN

Rule #1: Never return a call a man makes to you at any time during the relationship. You don't want to look desperate. Should you see him in public, and he asks you about calls he has made, run off to hang out with your friends before he can speak with you further. Men love busy, unattainable, and popular women. Be the woman he can't get, and he'll pursue you to the ends of the earth.

Rule #2: Never let a man know what you like. He will invariably use that to manipulate you. Even if you love flowers, should you receive some from him, throw them in the gutter after you smell them. If he gets upset, say, "I smell them once, and then throw them away. That's just me!" This keeps you safe from male manipulative tactics.

Rule #3: During your second date, tell your man that you come from a long line of knife throwers. Let him know that you wish to demonstrate your skills on him. If he backs off, he wasn't really interested in you in the first place, and you should find someone else.

Rule #4: After the third date, take a six-week trip to a foreign country and forget to tell him about it. When you return, if he is still interested, you know you are dating someone who is serious about you.

Rule #5: Two months into the relationship, start speaking a different language entirely, such as Swedish. If a man still wants to be with you, he will learn whatever language you are now speaking. If he doesn't, or can't, he was never meant to be in your life.

Rule #6: If he has successfully made it to the third month, let him begin to touch you. While holding hands is the preferred place to start, the more risqué woman may consider allowing him to put his arm around her waist.

Rule #7: If a man takes you to a romantic location, bends down on one knee, presents you with a ring, and asks for your hand in marriage, be aware that he is just kidding and that this is just a test to see if you know the kind of proposal a real woman deserves. Were he genuinely serious, he would invite you to a sporting event and put his big question on the scoreboard during the game. That's what real men do, and what real women respond to.

~~~

RULES FOR MEN

Rule #1: Men should make at least a half a million dollars a year before even starting the dating process. If that means you don't start dating until you are fifty, so be it. Financial preparation is always the first step.

Rule #2: A single man should never own a phone. It only makes him look desperate. If a woman really wants to get in touch with a man, she will come over to his home. She will respect the lack of a phone on his part as a sign of power and good boundaries.

Rule #3: If a woman criticizes or tries to rearrange any article of your clothing, it means she doesn't like you. End the relationship immediately.

Rule #4: Stay aloof. Never share your emotional self or deepest side, even after marriage. Whatever you do, don't become her soul mate. Stay distant. Women are attracted to men who are distant and unknowable. Familiarity breeds contempt. Therefore, a complete lack of knowledge of the other person will lead to undying devotion. Women know an aloof man is strong and dependable. They also know they will be the only one in the relationship to talk about feelings, which means they'll have the monopoly on that area, and this makes them happy.

Rule #5: Keep things mysterious. Don't tell the woman in your life what you do for a living, even after tying the knot. This way, she'll wonder if you work for the FBI or some other dangerous organization and worry about whether you will come home at the end of the day. She will give you a passionate kiss each morning when you leave and tell you to be safe. If she knew you were a computer programmer for a stuffed toy company, she would not have the same excitement about your departure and return. Now and then, disappear for months at a time with no explanation, and when you return, just say you were on "special assignment" and that you were "lucky to get out alive." She'll just be glad to have you back and look at you with awe.

Rule #6: When you get home from work each day, pretend to have forgotten her name and the kids' names. She'll understand completely, as you have put your life on the line all day, and she'll sit on your lap and say, "Honey, it's me, remember?" and kiss you and stroke your hair. Thus your relationship can begin anew each day.

Rule #7: Don't send text messages during lovemaking. Ideally, keep all forms of wireless communications devices off the bed. Your partner deserves your complete attention during private times, and this requires both your hands. You can only text during intimate moments if you tell her it concerns an ongoing surveillance operation you can't discuss. Then texting may be an acceptable part of the mystique you've created.

I could see I had done everything completely wrong with Kelly. I had opened up too much to her. She knew what I did for a living. She knew where I went every day. There was no mystery left about me. I would have to create some.

Overall, the seminar was amazing. Finally, I had the guidelines to help us keep the relationship going. But as incredible as the seminar was, it was information I needed a long time ago. Kelly was gone. I had just not been mysterious enough, plus I had let her get to know me intimately, not to mention a lot of other rules I had broken as well. At least I realized that if Kelly came back, I would have to tell her I had a new job, but I couldn't tell her what it was. I wasn't too happy, though, about the idea of having to wait three months to put my arms around her again. But rules are rules, and we would have to follow them if we wanted to be a couple.

I got home and turned on the TV, and started watching, *A Large Portion of the Population Likes Tyrone*. I loved watching this show. It had a good-natured feel that made me believe I was part of their family.

As I watched the show and saw Tyrone, a washed-up professional wrestler, argue with his beautiful wife Belinda, I realized why Kelly hadn't come back to me. It wasn't that I lacked mystery. It was because I wasn't as virile as Tyrone. He didn't have a job, had terrible table manners, was always scheming some new plan to get rich, and kept getting into trouble with his best friend, a Bushman named !Kung, who had just moved to America from Africa. Despite all his failings, however, Tyrone was manly enough to keep a stunning wife like Belinda in his orbit. The reason was simple: he exuded testosterone. I needed to become as manly a man as he was.

I thought about all the boyfriends Kelly told me she dated before we got together. The biker who was always on the road and whom she saw once a month. The muscle-bound sculptor who lived and worked all day in the nude in his studio. The ex-NFL lineman who barely talked to her and just grunted at the table when he wanted more food. They were all real men. And here I was, Mr. Nice Guy, a yard worker, a man whose toughest enemy was a pile of leaves and a gust of wind. I guess it's amazing she stayed with me as long as she did.

Kelly had even called me a soft male the day she left. This was the key. I was sure of it. If I could fix this, I knew I had a chance of attracting her back.

I thought immediately of the best place to go to become a true, hairy, manly man: the week-long seminar in the woods with the manliest of men, Wendell Vance, author of *From Wimps to Winners*. I packed my bags and left for Oregon the following Friday.

Two Weeks

Wendell Vance

For a man constantly to seek safety is dangerous.
        —Wendell Vance

There is an epidemic of soft males today, and all of you men are soft or you wouldn't be here," Wendell Vance barked at us. He was dressed in animal skins and standing on a tree stump, holding a drum, while we sat on the ground in the middle of an Oregon forest looking up at him. "And I am here to turn you into real men. I am a real, savage man, and you will all be as real and as savage as me one day—if you are lucky. This week is the beginning of that journey." I looked at his high cheekbones, his tall, muscular frame, his swarthy complexion, and the steel gaze that seemed to look right through us all. I wondered how I could get this same barbaric vigor and confidence myself.

"A woman becomes a woman automatically," Wendell said,

"because nature just makes it happen. But a man has to be built, step by step. And who builds men today? Nobody! And that's the problem. How many of you are mama's boys?"

Each of the men sheepishly raised his hand.

"That's right, you all are. But we're going to change that."

We all cheered.

"Now, you know what makes a man soft?" Wendell asked. "He's hiding behind something. The question is, behind what? We're going to find out for each of you. Why don't you expose yourselves fully to the world and become a man while you still can? What are you crouching behind—your mama? Well, your mama ain't here to save you. Your girlfriend? She ain't here either. How about your job? For this week, none of you has a job, a wardrobe, a relationship, or even a label. Whatever mask you wear out there, none of it is going to work here. We are systematically going to take away everything you are hiding behind this week, and let you explore and glory in what is underneath. By the end, you'll leave here a real man. And none of you better be gay!"

There was a silence.

"Any gay men out there?" he bellowed, and it echoed through the forest. No one answered as he looked around at each of us.

"That's good," he said, "because a gay man can never really be a full, manly man. Do you know why? Because to be a social success around other men, a man only has to be a boy. But to be around a woman, and fully captivate her, a man has to become a man. That's where the work is. And that's why we need to be grateful to women. Without them, we might never become men. And to help you become men, I want to introduce you to one of your lead instructors for the week, Belle Ulanda. She's more manly than many of you, I'm sure."

Bounding onto another tree stump came the tall, brunette, statuesque Belle. We all looked around, surprised that one of our teachers on manhood was a woman. She gave us a martial arts demonstration, made fire from pine needles and twigs, as we were going to have to learn to do, and then told us about all the activities planned for the week ahead.

We then split up into groups of eight, and went out into the woods to make tools out of whatever we could find. The goal was to spend the day hunting with these homemade tools. Our group didn't fare well. We had an accountant, an audio engineer, a shoe salesman, a surfer, and other men with no background in hunting or tool-making. When dinnertime came, we returned empty-handed, while other groups had caught and killed rabbits, deer, and squirrels. We didn't eat dinner that night as a punishment for our inability to fashion any weapons. Wendell told our group that hunger sharpens your hunting skills, and we would do well the next day.

"You will learn," Wendell shouted to the group as a whole, "that you have to go out and get for yourself in this world or you'll go hungry. Just because you went to college or your daddy got you a nice job at the firm doesn't mean anything out here, and it won't help you become a real man, either."

That night, hungry as our unfed group was, we banged on drums with our hands until we were exhausted, and then fell asleep on the forest floor.

We awoke the next morning to the sound of Wendell blowing on a conch shell. We ate a breakfast of dried meat, after which Belle led us through the woods on a five-mile run. We then gathered for another day of lectures and activities. We were told that for the remainder of the day we could communicate only through grunting. We had to put all our feelings and energy into our grunts and grimaces so that our meaning was clear. Wendell said that language was invented by women, and made you "soft" because it had no animal energy and made you explain things, when manhood was based on "doing."

By the third day, our group had at last figured out how to hunt well enough to catch something, and we were finally able to eat dinner. We also learned how to make fire from twigs and pine needles to cook our food.

On the fourth day, we were taught more manly rituals, painted our faces with pigments we made from the earth, and swam in a mountain lake Wendell led us to.

The last night, Saturday night, was the toughest. We had to crawl through the tunnel of fire. It was a tunnel made from the branches of thorny bushes, and it was set on fire as we crawled through it to let us know there was no turning back. When I got to the end of it, bloodied and tired, I felt like a changed man, and knew I had overcome something and left many soft parts of myself behind as I met the screaming and ecstatic faces of my male friends cheering me on.

As I said good-bye to everyone, and put on my regular clothes, I didn't want to wash off my face paint. In a sense, I realized it would always be there. I really learned something from Wendell and Belle and the rest of his staff in the woods. This was one week that had not been a waste of time. I didn't know if I felt like a complete, hairy man, but I had taken a big step in that direction, and the rest of the journey to manhood would be easier now that I knew which way to go.

No wonder Kelly had left me, I thought, on the plane ride home. I was convinced she was gone for good now. Who would want to be with any man who had not crawled through the tunnel of fire? Even though I knew she was probably not coming back, I somehow felt freer and happier. Everything seemed to matter less. I guess that is what crawling through a long tube of burning branches will do to you.

Two Weeks

Meeting Master Lohan

Succeed at failure, and fail at success.
—Master Lohan

Three weeks after the Wendell Vance seminar, and after catching up on all the weeding and seeding work that had gotten backlogged, I stopped in front of the window of an arts and crafts store in Manhattan and thought about Wendell Vance and the face paints. I missed them and the power they gave me. Just then, a white Rolls Royce drove up Park Avenue and I was reminded of the money I had sent to Umberto Slidell. I turned onto 48th Street and saw a vegetable stand, and thought of Repak and his magical tureen. I was doing my best not to make any mistakes, had not touched the lava, and had actually asked someone how to use a fax machine at an office supply store. I tried not to fall into Calmness Syndrome, and if I found myself in that state, I would jar myself out of it with a candy bar. Everything seemed to be working OK. I had really enjoyed most of the seminars. But something still seemed to be missing.

I then took a weekend Mindfulness Training Course in the apartment of an experienced Buddhist woman in Manhattan. Twelve of us meditated for an hour, and then walked around the city looking at homeless people. We were cautioned by our teacher not to give them any money—it was enough to be aware of their plight and open our hearts in compassion to them as we walked on by. At the end of the weekend, we were each given a degree certifying us as Counselors of Buddhist Mindfulness. I didn't love the course, but at least I got a certificate, which no other course had given me, and I felt ready to share what I had learned.

That afternoon, I walked into a used bookstore in Greenwich Village and went over to the self-help section. There had to be someone else, I thought, one more person, someone with a real message who could make a difference in who I was. Maybe someone before my time had written a better book, so I figured a used bookstore might lead me to them. I looked over all the authors, and knew nearly all of them. I was about to leave, when I looked in a box that someone had just dropped off. I asked the owner of the store if I could look through the box, and he said sure, but that he was just going to throw out what was in there, as they were not very good books. In it I found a series of old, tattered paperbacks by an author I had never heard of, someone called Master Lohan. I flipped through a badly worn copy of his out-of-print book, *I'm OK, You're Not OK*. As I started reading it, I began to be intrigued. I then read the first chapter of *How to Lose Friends and Alienate People*, and was surprised to learn that Master Lohan did not care what effect you or he had on the world. His ideas about personal growth were the opposite of what I had read so far. I pulled his other books out of the box, such as *People Who Love Too Much and Why They Drive Me Up A Wall* and *Do What You Love and the Money Won't Follow*. I ended up leaving with a worn copy of his longest book, *The Eight Habits of Highly Ineffective People*. I went home and finished it by early morning. Instead of trying to fit in and accomplish things, Master Lohan said you should do your best to be as complete a failure as possible, and to fit in nowhere. Being ineffective came naturally to me, and was what I was always good at. Finally, a book that said failure was the true path. I felt my real journey was beginning.

To save you the trouble of finding a copy, here are Lohan's eight habits, guaranteed to make you highly ineffective in no time at all:

1. Tell everyone the truth.
2. If you don't like your job, quit.
3. Spend three hours alone every day.
4. Lose contact with those you don't like.
5. Always take the slowest form of transportation.
6. Don't watch television.

7. Don't read the newspaper.
8. Sleep on the floor.

My favorite moment was when Master Lohan wrote, "If one cannot be appropriate, it is very important to be as inappropriate as possible." That was it—I had spent too much time in my life trying to fit in when I had always been out of place in any situation in which I had found myself. I felt I had at last found my true teacher.

I went back to the used bookstore the next day, and asked the man about Master Lohan. I was eager to know why he was so unknown. The clerk told me Master Lohan never did much to promote his books, and that when he did go on TV and radio, he did everything wrong. He staged a Worldwide Day of Mindfulness for Hunger the same day as the Coney Island hot dog-eating contest. He started a bottled water company that charged $10,000 per bottle, of which $9,999.50 went to relieve water shortages in poor communities. He founded a Buddhist pest control company where the workers removed each bug by hand and released them outside alive. It lost him a lot of money. He then called National Public Radio "the Great Satan" in a television interview. No one showed any interest in Master Lohan after that. His books stopped being reviewed or recognized by anyone.

I found out that Master Lohan lived in Las Vegas, and spent his time selling Buicks by day and lecturing to local meditation groups by night. I flew to see him a week later. Everyone on the plane was upbeat about gambling or whatever other fun they had planned. I kept wondering, as we flew across the desert and made our final approach, had I made the right choice? Perhaps flying out west to try to meet someone I didn't know was nuts. But something pulled me toward Master Lohan, and it was too late now to turn back.

The following morning, I left my hotel in a cab headed for The Gun Store at 2900 East Tropicana Avenue, where Master Lohan was known to spend a lot of time. I rented a Smith & Wesson revolver, bought fifty rounds, got fitted with ear protection, and walked into the shooting range. I shot off my rounds, looked over, and there he was. He was shooting off a Belgian submachine gun and admiring the smoothness of its action, stroking it gently after each few rounds. Clearly, he was experienced with guns. I knew him instantly from his long dark ponytail, his wise Asian countenance, his tan sandals that seemed to have traveled the world, and the "Hello My Name is Master Lohan" badge that he wore from the New Age conference he was attending that weekend. I will never forget the first words I heard him say:

"Those Belgians. Makers of smooth chocolates and smoother submachine guns."

I instantly knew I was in the presence of someone very special.

I bought another fifty rounds, shot them off, and waited for Master Lohan to finish. We then began to talk and I told him how much I liked *The Eight Habits of Highly Ineffective People*. We went for coffee, and in the space of five short hours, I had told him my life story. I told him about Kelly and how I hoped she would come back.

The conversation then wandered onto the topic of feminists. I told him I did not know what was now considered appropriate male-female behavior in the post-feminist era. He said that few women were completely feminist anymore: they were more likely to be half-feminist. He said that if I date a woman who is half-feminist, when the bill comes, I should pay three-quarters of it. If a woman is two-thirds feminist, I should pay two-thirds of the bill, because two-thirds of one-half is one-third of the whole. He also said that if a woman is only fifty percent feminist, I should hold the door open halfway and let her open it the rest of the way. He said dating quasi-feminists can be tricky, but as long as I brought along a calculator, or could do fractions quickly in my head, I would be fine.

We then went to a casino and played cards, just the two of us. He continued to teach me things I did not know, especially about poker. I had two pair, and then he laid down a 2, 4, 6, 8, and 10. He said it was a Cincinnati Straight, which is any straight that skips in twos, and that it beats two pair. He collected the money. The next hand I had three nines, and thought he was bluffing, so the bidding went high. He laid down all diamonds and hearts in random order. I went to collect the pot, and he stopped me. He said that what he had was called a Kansas City Flush, which is any hand that is all a single color, and that it beats three of a kind. Finally, for the biggest pot of the day, I had a full house. I put my last dollar in to see his hand. Master Lohan laid down a 3, 5, 7, jack, and king. Again, I reached for the money and he stopped me. He said he had what is called a Prime, which is only prime-numbered cards and is a very rare hand that easily beats a full house. I lost everything I came with, but discovered unknown hands of poker and how the game is truly played. I looked forward to using this newfound knowledge when I played with a larger group.

Our conversation during the game was more valuable than any money I lost. Upon hearing about my quest for personal growth since losing Kelly, he said that I would never become enlightened anyway, and that I should give up on it, embrace my ego, and just have a good time. He said there was a lot in life you could just ignore or deny, and by doing so, make your life a lot more enjoyable. He said that for me the thing to try to avoid was any quest toward higher consciousness. He said I would just be wasting my time anyway. I felt he was right.

We walked along the streets of Las Vegas after playing, and he turned to me and asked, "So, Kincaid, do you want to study with me?"

"Sure," I said.

"All right," he said, "time for initiation."

"What do we do?" I asked.

He pulled a pack of Starburst candy out of his pocket. He

opened it up and I looked at all the colored square candies.

"Pick a flavor," he said.

I looked at them carefully, and picked strawberry. He asked me to pick another, and I picked lemon.

"OK," he said, taking a slingshot out of his pocket. "Go across the street and I will shoot it up in the air. If you catch it in your mouth, we go forward. Otherwise, we go our separate ways and pretend we never met."

"Do I have to catch one of these two, or that's it?"

"No," he said, "we do it until you catch it. But always pretend you only have once chance."

I walked across the street and watched him unwrap the strawberry Starburst and put it in the slingshot. I bent my knees a little and looked up into the bright sky. He shot the Starburst high over the passing cars, and it came right at me, but as I ran to get under it, it bounced off my cheek. I got ready again. He shot the lemon one higher over the wires and the traffic, giving the candy more air time, and me a better chance to catch it. This time it bounced off my chin. He took out another one, and paused for a moment as I got ready, then shot that one. It hit me in the forehead. This went on for quite awhile. He must have shot off three packs. The ground around me was littered with the colorful candies. He walked across the street. He didn't look happy as he dodged the traffic and made his way over to me.

"Why are you moving?" he asked.

"So I can get under it," I said.

"You're already under it."

"Well, I just figured—"

"Don't figure. Just stand here. And don't move. Now close your eyes."

I did as he said. He walked back. I felt people staring at me as I stood there waiting with my mouth open.

I waited.

And waited.

I then heard the sound of his slingshot go off.

Five seconds later I felt a square candy land right on my tongue. I started chewing slowly. It tasted like real strawberries. I started thinking about Kelly, and how she had taken me out to meet her parents in Northern California the month after we met. They ran a strawberry farm. She said it was strawberry season and we had to go visit. She showed me all around the area, and took me to Point Lobos to watch the seals and sea lions. We went to the aquarium in Carmel, where she used to volunteer, and she gave me the grand tour. We then had a nice dinner with her family, and then Kelly led me into the barn for dessert. She had a box of organic strawberries she had picked that morning. She said I could only eat them if I caught them in my mouth. We sat down, and she threw them one by one, and I caught most of them. They tasted like the first real strawberries I had ever eaten. Maybe it was the sea air, or because they were allowed to ripen in the fields. But each strawberry had the taste of ten of those we ate in New Jersey. I felt like one of those strawberries was exploding in my mouth right now, not candy.

I opened my eyes and Master Lohan was standing next to me.

"You know, Kincaid, if you stand still, you'll find a lot more things come to you."

"Sure," I said.

"You must be hungry. Want to try the buffet at the Bellagio? Best in town. They have a great green bean almondine. You like string beans? I don't think anyone knows what they are doing with string beans anymore."

We headed off to the Bellagio, and talked about everything and anything as we watched the tourists and gamblers pass us on the street. He started talking about the next book he was working on, a novel, and said that since no one read novels anymore, he was thinking of going straight to CliffsNotes.

When we got to the buffet, I asked Master Lohan if he had any rules for those who studied with him.

"Yes," he said. "First rule is, I am not opposed to you laughing when you find something funny. Okay?"

"Sure," I said.

"Second, I am not opposed to you resting when you are tired. All right?"

"Okay," I said.

"Third, I am not opposed to you eating when you are hungry. Hungry?"

"You bet," I said.

"So get a plate and fill it up," he said. "Everything is wonderful here."

As we sat eating, I asked him a lot of questions, though I couldn't understand half his answers. He was right about the string beans, though. They were incredibly flavorful. Not overcooked, and with a hint of almond. Everything at the Bellagio buffet tasted amazing. We ate for a while, and then I said,

"You know, Master Lohan, there's only one thing."

"What?" he said.

"There are things I wish I hadn't said to Kelly. I wish I could take them back. Can things ever be undone?"

"No," he said, nodding. "Not possible."

"Why not?" I asked.

"Because nothing can ever be done in the first place." He then went back to eating his string beans.

I didn't understand. We had done a lot today. What did he mean nothing happened? I thought everything happened today. I thought everything was finally beginning.

Two Weeks

Master Lohan's Effect Upon My Work

You can't change people. You can only make them more of who they already are. –Master Lohan

After meeting Master Lohan, I went home and felt inspired about writing again. I didn't need Paul and Vinnie. I was motivated on my own now. I tried writing movie scripts. I had always liked being part of great traditions, so all the scripts I wrote in the weeks that followed were either sequels or prequels to preexisting classics.

I started writing about Rocky Balboa, a film character I greatly admired. My first script was *Rocky VII*. In *Rocky VII*, Rocky passes away. Two weeks prior to his death, he had signed on to a title fight. His manager, played magically by Burgess Meredith, decides to go on with the fight. They put the casket on wheels, and keep pushing it at his opponent, who wears himself out trying to punch the casket into submission. Finally, Burgess pushes the casket into the opponent so hard it knocks him down and Rocky wins.

I then wrote a script for *Rocky VIII*. This time Rocky has been cremated. A rival fighter goes on television saying that Rocky is all washed up now that he's been turned into ashes, and that his punches have nothing left. This angers his manager, again played by Burgess Meredith, and they arrange a fight. Burgess picks up the urn in the dressing room right before the fight, wraps it in white fighter tape, looks at it, and says, "We've only got one shot here, Rock, so let's make it count." In the first round, Burgess taunts the opposing fighter with the urn, and then throws the ashes in the fighter's face, blinding him. The fighter falls to the canvas, it's declared a TKO, and Rocky triumphs again.

Both scripts had a deeply spiritual message. Rocky was determined to fight beyond his abilities to achieve his goal. Being dead didn't slow him down or put him in a bad mood. It didn't get in his way of being the best fighter he knew he could be, and coming home with the title each time. I couldn't find anyone interested in the scripts, however.

I then worked up a script for *The Penultimate Mohican*, a promising prequel, but it became another piece no one wanted. I decided I had neither the talent nor connections to write movies and decided to stick to yard work.

But something deeper was tugging at me now. It was clear to me that I needed to do more than just move leaves around. I fell in with a rebel group of librarians in New Jersey that wanted to create a revolution in the country by carrying out a radical act. Their plan was to secretly rearrange the alphabet on January 1, and, by doing so, bring America to her knees. I met their leader, a religious man named Zabreki, who said that Z should now come first, citing the Bible phrase that "the last will be first and the first will be last." Zabreki said he didn't like sitting in the back of all his classes in high school, and wanted his kids to sit up front and learn more than he did. Another faction wanted all the vowels at the beginning, and another group wanted to eliminate all silent letters. I eventually stopped going to the meetings because I found them too disorganized.

I then decided simply to start to teach others about denial. I volunteered to teach after-school classes at our local elementary school, and taught fourth-graders how to avoid doing homework. I told them the key was to simply say, "No comment" or "I have no comment at this time" when asked by their teacher where their work was. Legally, they didn't have to say anything else. The kids loved it, and said they would use it very soon. At last I felt I was doing something meaningful in the world with what I had learned from Master Lohan.

Two Weeks

We All Use Denial

Cigarettes don't kill you, death does.
—Cigarette industry spokesperson

Spending time with **Master Lohan** made me realize what I had suspected after reading his books: that he had long ago mastered denial, and that was the secret to his happiness. He believed that there was rarely, if ever, a need to face things head-on. I felt a joy when he told me this, and denial then became the centerpiece of the spiritual practice that I would soon share with others. Surprisingly, the more I studied his teachings, the more I found that I, too, had the gifts to become a spiritual teacher and guide. It seemed to come out of nowhere. It started first with answering simple questions at gardening clubs and hardware stores, and spread from there.

The first thing I tell everyone is that we all use denial regularly. For example, we may sit on a street corner consuming a beverage covered with a paper bag because we do not wish passersby to know the contents of the bottle we are drinking from. We may buy something on credit with the full knowledge that we can never truly afford it, yet we enjoy it until it is repossessed. We may slip our dentist an extra twenty bucks, asking him to ignore any cavities he finds. While all of these behaviors were frowned upon in the past, they are no longer, for we are living in the Age of Denial.

Here are the Five Stages of Denial that nearly all of us go through, which I have taken from Master Lohan's out-of-print book, *Let's Not and Say We Did: Using Denial to Get the Job and Life You Want:*

The Five Stages of Denial
1. Denial.
2. Denial that one is in denial.
3. Pretending to be unaware of the denial of one's denial.
4. A lack of recognition of the ever-widening gap between oneself and reality.
5. A job at the State Department.

Another way we use denial is when we move into a new home or apartment and "redecorate." The walls may be blue, and we proceed to paint them yellow. We then believe they are truly yellow, when underneath we know they are still blue.

Other ways we all engage in denial every day:

- *Really Simple* magazine is over 700 pages long.
- We buy fennel-flavored toothpaste and act as though we like it because we paid seven dollars for it.
- We deny any connection to our government even though, technically, it is ours.

WE ARE WEALTHY BEYOND OUR DREAMS

One of the things we deny about ourselves is that we have endless riches we never use. We act as though we are poor, and that we need to look to others to fill our needs, but this is not the case. Everything we need we already possess. We only need to connect to what we have and bring it to life.

There is the well-known fable of a beggar sitting on the street with a million dollars in his pocket. His wealth can be plainly seen by others, but not himself. Even though he possesses great riches, he keeps asking passersby for change. Finally, a passerby says, "But you are not poor—I can see that you have a great fortune in your pocket." The beggar says, "When I say change, I don't mean a handout, I mean change for a hundred, which no one has. And, no bank will allow me to come in wearing these dirty, smelly clothes. Because of that, I continue to starve." Eventually, since no one carries enough change, the beggar dies on the street. The spiritual message of this story is simple: we should all carry change for a hundred.

We can all relate to this story personally. We all possess riches, but cannot access them because no one gives change to strangers on the street anymore. But there is an even bigger message here: we need to anticipate the needs of others. Had someone merely thought to bring change for a hundred that day, the beggar could have lived a full and rich life. Such forethought is necessary if we are to truly call ourselves compassionate and help those around us who have yet to actualize all that they possess.

But I don't have a million dollars. How does this story apply to me?

You must realize that in this story a million dollars is a metaphor for the riches we all possess.

So, I need someone to change my riches for me so I can use them?

No, and that is the best news of all: you don't need to change anything about yourself. You are perfect the way you are.

Two Weeks

There is another story that illustrates a similar point. It is the story of the man who cannot find his cow. He walks around his town looking for her, and travels a great distance all around the countryside in India, asking, "Have you seen my cow?" He describes her in detail. Everyone says no. He arrives home distraught. Then, he hears a sound from the basement and discovers that his cow has been waiting for him the whole time. He then buys a shotgun and shoots the cow, because he is angry at the cow for having made him waste so much time. He then regrets shooting the cow, goes into gestalt therapy, and finds out that the cow's absence brought up abandonment issues he had with his parents who dropped him off at an orphanage when he was five. He is then unable to pay for therapy because his cow was his only source of income. Thus he fails to find the riches inside himself.

The message of this story is simple: before going into any kind of therapy, make sure to have enough money set aside so that you can completely mine the riches inside you.

WHAT IS MY PURPOSE IN LIFE?

Many people seek happiness by trying to find their purpose in life. But happiness may come from realizing that you do not have a purpose. The real danger is to convince yourself, either after reading a book or attending a seminar, that you have some grand purpose in this world when you really don't. By falsely believing you do, you attach yourself to an incorrect purpose, only to discover at the end of your life that you really did not have this purpose to begin with and that you wasted your own and everyone else's time with it. You ended up doing something you had no business doing. Worse, had you realized you had no purpose from the beginning, you could have done nothing but enjoy yourself your whole life instead of slaving away at some arbitrary goal. In addition, all that activity and travel burns fossil fuels, which in turn causes global warming.

ACCEPTING THE PURPOSELESS LIFE

Master Lohan, both in his teachings and in his long-forgotten book, *The Purposeless Life*, reminded me of this teaching every day I was with him: if you think you have a purpose, you may be wrong. You may not have one. But if you don't have a purpose, this is good news, because you can have a really good time and not worry about anything. Having fun, he often said, can be your purpose.

Your real mission in life may be to not have a purpose. This can be the greatest calling of all. You will be a blessing to so many around you who feel trapped inside the need to "have a purpose." You can help set them free. You will be setting an example by not having one, and will help them realize there is no point to their existence either except to have fun. Such an insight can come as a great relief to many, take a load off their backs, and significantly increase their chances of experiencing their own lives.

Another important part of this teaching, Master Lohan said, was to make sure you are not being selfless when deep down you are selfish. Those who wrongly suppress their selfishness are particularly susceptible to picking up false purposes. Meditation, he said, is an excellent way to get in touch with your inner selfishness and liberate yourself from the illusion of selflessness.

Two Weeks

MISERY IS SHARED UNIVERSALLY

We may deny misery, but the misery of even one person can have dramatic effects on us all. The unhappiness of only one person in a city can lower the mood of the entire area. For example, should but one person in a large city set off an atomic bomb to express his or her negative energy, we can all "feel" their emotions even though we have never met this person. Thus, without even interacting, we are intimately aware of his or her feelings and how they can affect us all.

Two Weeks

Mindfulness

Why does the Air Force need expensive new bombers? Have the people we've been bombing over the years been complaining? –George Wallace

THE POWER OF MINDFULNESS

In order to understand the world, we need to slow our minds down and quiet them so we can see what is in front of us. Much of our confusion about the world results from our attempt to decide what we are experiencing before we actually experience it. In *The Eight Habits of Highly Ineffective People,* Master Lohan quotes British author James Burke: "For things to make sense, you have to make up your mind about them in advance." Yet this is a mistake, Master Lohan says. If we truly wish to see the world around us, we must first fully remove all the preconceived notions in our head. We cannot make up our minds in advance. We must quiet all our thoughts. Only then can we really see what is in front of us. This is mindfulness.

Mindfulness decides nothing and adds nothing. It simply experiences what is there without bringing anything additional to it. Think of the universe as a beautiful Bach cantata. Our mind is like a kazoo that wants to play along and constantly add its own part. It wants to add its noise to everything we experience. The goal with mindfulness is to silence the kazoo and experience the beautiful music around us in its most pristine and pure form: its unadorned form. Mindfulness, then, is simply silencing your mind's kazoo.

My first experience with mindfulness occurred during the first week I spent with Master Lohan, watching him sell used cars using the power of mindfulness in Las Vegas. A customer would get in a car and ask, "What is so unique about this convertible?" He would answer in his mesmerizing voice, "This is a very special car. You see this steering wheel? If you turn it to the right, the car goes to the right. If you turn it to the left, it goes to the left. This car will go anywhere you want. Just press the accelerator, and you can go as fast as you want." The customer would become entranced and usually buy the car. The idea of a car that could take you anywhere you wanted was too hard to resist. No wonder Master Lohan was the number-one Buick salesman in Las Vegas.

From this firsthand experience of the power of mindfulness, and also by reading every spiritual book I could acquire on the topic, I tried to incorporate mindfulness and my full presence into my life. I read *I and Thou* by Martin

Buber, and tried to have an I-Thou relationship with my toast. When I did that, I realized I didn't have an I-Thou relationship with Kelly. Maybe I had an I-hair relationship with her, or an I-eyes relationship, or an I-body relationship, but not an I-Thou relationship. That may have been the biggest problem of all.

UNDERSTANDING THE WORLD WITH MINDFULNESS

One of my first experiences with mindfulness involved trying to understand this trademarked phrase of the Fox News Organization:

We report. You decide.

The first time I heard it, I was sitting in the Greyhound bus station in Kansas City, Missouri at 7 a.m., bleary-eyed from an all-night bus ride through Kansas on my way back from visiting Master Lohan in Las Vegas. I sat there and watched the TV monitor, and mulled it over in my head.

We report. You decide.

The phrase was going by too quickly. I closed my eyes. I took a deep breath. I tried to break it down:

We report.

I stayed with that part of it for a while. I breathed slowly. I was beginning to understand. They report. It made sense that they would report, they being a news organization and all.

I then said the second half:

You decide.

We decide? What do we decide? Which countries to invade? Where to spend our tax dollars? Which species, if any, to save? I understood that they reported, but I didn't think there was anything that we decided. The age of Americans actually deciding anything was over. Except maybe what to have for dinner. If you had enough money for dinner.

I then dozed off for a while, waiting for the connecting bus to St. Louis. I started to dream about other establishments achieving the same level of terse summary in their slogans as Fox News:

Rick's Diner: *We Cook, You Eat.*
Bob Jones University: *We Teach, You Learn.*
Internal Revenue Service: *You Earn, We Take.*

USING MINDFULNESS IN OUR EVERYDAY LIVES

I realized that there are many people who do not use mindfulness in their everyday lives. The most glaring example in our community is our local fire department here in Red Bank, New Jersey. I realized this when I arrived home. I went over and talked with them one afternoon, and mentioned that instead of being in such a rush when they get a call, they should put their gear on *mindfully*, being aware of what they are doing, slowly putting on each glove, boot, and coat. It would take longer, but they would be fully conscious of the experience of being a fireman when the day was over. Their life spent fighting fires would no longer be a blur. As Master Lohan says, if you do not do something mindfully, you are not doing it at all in a true sense.

Just then, a call came in, and everything I had just shared with them was completely thrown out the window. They threw their gear on in a hurry, abandoned their lunch, and headed off. "Where's the fire?" I yelled at them sarcastically as they pulled out in three trucks. I followed in my car, and saw that the blaze was just up the street from me, at my neighbor's house.

I stood with my neighbor and watched his house burn to the ground. He looked at the flames destroying all his memories as his wife and kids stood by his side. I tried to tell him that his "house" and "possessions" were merely a story he was telling himself, and that none of this was real. He just looked at me, obviously upset. But I feel that the truth will sink in with him and one day he will see that I am right. The only reason my friend was upset was that he was too invested in whatever his mind was telling him at that particular moment, and believing the story in his consciousness. He is still rich beyond measure, even though he did not have the foresight to renew his fire insurance.

Showing a lack of mindfulness, he then asked me if he and his wife and children could stay at my house that night. I said no. I didn't want them going through my house, especially with their smoky hair smelling like burning wood and plastics. That stuff is toxic. That smell would take days to get out of the house, and might never come out of the pillows. They have an aunt who lives nearby, and I suggested they stay with her. It is probably best for them to get away from this scene, which is filled with so many memories, and not wake up tomorrow and try to salvage what is left. Doing so would just be a way to stay attached to a reality that was never really "real" in the first place. He needs to just move on, and staying here would not help him do that. Therefore, my selfishness is really a spur to his personal growth, and one day he will thank me for that.

Two Weeks

Your Questions and Answers

Be careful of whom you are trying to make happy.
—Master Lohan

After studying with Master Lohan, and developing my own unique system of denial while working as a full-time lawn worker, many people have come up to me at feed stores, gardening shops, and nurseries, asking me questions about denial and related matters. I have included their questions and answers here because they are likely to be the same ones you will have. I hope this section will help you deepen your knowledge of how to put things off indefinitely, and help you experience the joy that will come about as a result.

Who or what is God?
A very old man with a long beard who is all-powerful, knows everything, has the best computer, and can go through any airport security without being checked.

How do you know there is a God?
Easy. When do you want the sun up, during the day or the night? Day. If it came up at night, it would be a total waste of daylight. When do you want the days to be warmer, winter or summer? Summer, of course. It wouldn't make sense if days were longer in winter. Plus, when do you want days to be shorter? Winter. When you're inside. It doesn't matter as much. And when do you want water to freeze, summer or winter? Winter. Because you want to go ice skating in the cold, and you want the lake melted in the summer so you can go swimming and cool off. We can clearly see God's design in all of this, and thus, proof of His existence.

If the universe is only 6,000 years old, how is it that we can see light from stars that are millions of light years away? Isn't that light millions of years old?
Because when God created the universe, He created the light on its way at the same time. Don't say it's not possible—if God can create galaxies, He can create those light beams on their way.

Why does God allow suffering?
He loves all the attention it gives Him.

How long did it take God to create the world?
Six days, but He waited two weeks after He got the idea so He could enjoy the peace and quiet just a little bit longer.

I am not comfortable with anything religious. Religion has created wars that have killed millions of people. I don't want to be involved.
Yes, but remember, it's infidels like you who are the first to be killed in such wars, so whether you like it or not, you're involved.

Does personal growth ever end?
Yes, when you turn sixty. From then on, whatever opinions you have are the absolute truth, and you can spend all your time telling them to everyone.

What is guilt?
An emotional control system invented by Jews. It came about in response to their up-and-down relationship with God throughout ancient history. Originally, it helped bring some Jews back to God. When God stopped sending prophets, Jews then used guilt to enjoy pleasure backwards, and also to control their offspring. Guilt was eventually leased out to other peoples throughout the world under specific licensing agreements. When anyone throughout the world experiences guilt, they owe a debt of gratitude—or guilt—to the Jews.

Does guilt serve any purpose?
Guilt allows one to get by with very few experiences in life, as one can keep reenacting the same things over and over and consider what should have been done. This means we don't

have to actually experience that much in life, and can simply replay everything in our heads endlessly. Theoretically, guilt used this way could solve global warming by greatly reducing human activity and the need for fossil fuels.

What is your opinion of sex before marriage?
It is essential for the continuation of the human race.

What is your opinion of sex after marriage?
It could lower the divorce rate dramatically.

Some say the recent World Series victories of the Red Sox, White Sox, and Phillies are a sign that the world is coming to an end. Is this true?
Only if the Cleveland Indians and Chicago Cubs also win soon. So, it looks like planet Earth will be around for a long, long time.

Do you have a history of mental illness?
Yes.

Could you describe it?
It is a two-volume leather-bound set I keep in my bookcase.

My friends are all in support groups overcoming their addictions. They're having deep, profound experiences and forming wonderful friendships. I would like to start this

process as well, but don't know where to begin. How do I get started?

First, find something to get addicted to. The best way to find an addiction that works for you is to look into your family history and see what your ancestors were addicted to. This is the addiction that will most likely work best for you.

What are Mormons?

Mormons are the Chicago Cub fans of the religious world. You know they are never going to win the big one, but you have to respect their right to root for whichever team they want. It's the American way.

The Book of Mormon has the phrase, "And It Came to Pass" over a thousand times. Could this really be God's writing?

It was His last book, so there is bound to be some repetition.

What is homophobia?

"Homo" means same and "phobia" means fear, so homophobia means fear of the same thing. Those with homophobia never wear two socks that are the same color or watch a movie twice.

My daughter is piercing many parts of her body with rings and studs. Should I be concerned?

Only after the twentieth piercing. Then ask her about the last time something pierced her heart. And ask her what it was—a book? A person? A movie?

My friend has been meditating for a year and a half now for about an hour a day. We're competitive and I want to beat him at it, but I'm just starting. If I meditate three hours a day compared to his one, will I pass him at some point in my overall spiritual awareness?
Yes, in around six months if my math is right.

Why was show business invented?
Most of the population is depressed and searching for meaning in life, while two percent of the population is happy and cheerful. Show business seeks to take this two percent of the population and spread their happiness to everyone else.

My husband collects coins and old train sets. He is obsessive about them and spends all his free time in the basement looking at them and playing with them. I feel he is avoiding intimacy with me and not being present with our children. Should I be concerned?
No. Your husband is building a valuable collection that can one day be sold for a great profit. While you and the children may not get to spend that much time with him, he is really considering your best interests and wants you to have a comfortable retirement.

Can peace marches prevent wars?
To a degree, yes, but a more practical long-term solution is needed. We cannot eliminate war with peace marches alone. Just as we have used farm subsidies to pay farmers not to grow crops, we need a peace subsidy to pay defense contractors not to build bombs. If we have fewer bombs, we will have fewer wars. Rich and powerful people want their money. I say let them have it. Let's just ask them to build yachts with it instead. Whatever the price of peace is, let's pay it.

The Buddha advised the middle path, but George Schultz has said that he who walks down the middle gets hit from both sides. Will a Buddhist get hit from both sides?
Yes, but this is a great way to stimulate spiritual growth.

Can you sum up Buddhism in one phrase?
Don't be clingy.

What is chess?
A game devised to keep the best minds of each era so busy that they do not solve any real-world problems. For example, one European leader, a former chess champion, when confronted at a press conference with a question about the rising homeless problem, suggested "Ruy Lopez."

My grandmother used to call her underwear her

unmentionables. *No one uses that word any more. Why not?*
I don't know.

I have a friend who found out she has only two weeks to live. What should she do?
Now is an excellent time to get a facelift, which will cheer her up and get her mind off things. Also, suggest she hire a personal stylist. At times like this, you want to make sure what you're wearing works well with the particular colors in your hospital room. You want to look your best for all those last visits you receive from loved ones traveling a great distance in order to leave that final good impression.

I am going through a tough time right now, and my friend said one of her favorite spiritual sayings is, "It is always darkest before the dawn." Is that true? If so, it sounds so hopeful to me.
It's not true. Astronomers tell us it is actually darkest many hours before dawn. So, you still have a ways to go before this difficult time is over. Sorry!

Do you ever use a leaf blower?
What kind of red-blooded lawn worker would use a leaf blower? It doesn't prove you can rake—it only shows you know how to point something at something else.

Which is better, a metal or plastic rake?
When I was coming up through the ranks, they were all metal, so there wasn't even a question. I've never used plastic, on principle.

What's wrong with plastic rakes?
They'll move the leaves, but they don't aerate the lawns as well.

Can you rake a lawn that has no leaves on it?
Yes. I get a strange look when I do this, but this actually stimulates the grass, and is good for aerating the soil. Think of it as a scalp massage for your lawn.

Can rakes be dangerous?
Yes. Not many people know that most Asian martial arts were actually created during the Lawn Maintenance Wars that occurred in Japan and China thousands of years ago and that their weapons were fashioned out of primitive rakes.

Two Weeks

How Can You Heal a Broken Heart?

Our whims are our only true possessions.
—Master Lohan

There is a saying among lawn workers: Being in love is like raking on a windy day. You are only fooling yourself if you think anything is under your control.

Romantic love is an illusion, but as illusions go, it's one of the best, if not the best. When you are in love, life feels glamorous and exciting. Your every action is important. Your lover calls you each morning and tells you what she ate for breakfast. You tell her what you ate. Then you wonder why you're not eating breakfast together anymore. Why does she only call? Why isn't she here? But still the sun shines brighter as you think of her. The song of the birds makes your heart sing. You think someone cares about every aspect of you. There's a fullness, even as you're all alone and consider the possibility that the loud snoring you heard over the phone as she spoke might mean she's cheating on you, but still there's something that thrills you deeply.

While romantic love is an illusion, ending this illusion can lead to terrible pain and heartache. If you are unable to get that person off your mind, perform the following three-part ritual. It will remove this person and his or her memory from your mind forever:

1. Subscribe to *Soap Opera Digest* and read it regularly. Soon you will realize that your troubles are no different from the imaginary woes of these fictional characters, except that yours are real and really hurt.
2. Move to Turkmenistan and organize a rebel group there that tries to overthrow the oppressive regime. Set up a constitutional republic, but one that only appears to have democratic elections. Once you and your group gain power, start to oppress others as the former regime did. Learn how a lack of common rights in a large population can lead to misery, especially among the poor. This large-scale misery that you inflict will be more profound than your lost romance, and witnessing it up close will help you to heal.
3. Convince a friend to attach you to an electric shock cord and jolt you every time you think of your lost love.

If none of these three approaches works, enter long-term

therapy with a therapist who has an uncertain grasp of the English language. In order to try to understand what you're saying, he or she will pay much more attention to you than other therapists, and this level of attention alone will give you the amount of caring you need to heal.

NO EXIT

Often, some of the heartache we feel in life is not from failed romances, but from interactions with our own relatives. I realized this one night when I dreamed I was dying. I saw a swirling tunnel of light above me, and felt I was being called up into it by the feeling of love, but at the top of the tunnel I saw all my relations. I then wanted to live, and asked for two more weeks, but God said no. I looked up into the tunnel again and saw all my relatives urging me forward with smiles, waving me upward. I looked around in desperation and finally cried out, "Do you have another tunnel?" I pointed out to the Creator that Manhattan has at least four tunnels going into it, so heaven could have at least seven. He agreed, and said He would look into it.

Two Weeks

You Are Not Your Brain

Sometimes we are bulls; sometimes we are pine needles floating across the water. –Master Lohan

Many people worship the brain and human intelligence. This is a mistake. After all, it was only in the last decade that humans figured out that wheels should be put on all luggage.

Some people even feel they *are* their brain. This is not so. Were it true, you wouldn't need your liver. When a relative calls from the hospital and asks for your liver, you usually turn them down. This is because you are not just your brain, but also your liver. Without your liver you could not live, and your relative was hoping you didn't know that. As a general rule, only donate organs you have two of, such as your kidneys. We were given two of certain organs so we could be generous. When we were given one, that means hold on to it. This is known as setting healthy boundaries.

Keep this handy organ donation chart on your fridge for reference:

OK to Donate (limit one)	Do Not Donate (leads to death)
Kidney	Brain
Testes	Heart
Lung	Liver
Spleen (you can live without)	Small intestine
Bone marrow (give parts now and then)	Pancreas
Blood (we make some regularly)	Your entire skin

If the same relative calls from the hospital and asks for your kidney, make a deal. If you don't like that relative, and he says you don't have to come to any more holidays at his house if you give him the kidney, let him have it. You are coming out ahead.

There is an additional message here as well: when we only have one of something, we should keep it, and jump up and down, holding it and saying *mine, mine, mine*. It is only when we have more than one of something that we can give the extra one away. This spiritual instruction is written directly into our bodies.

Some religions say we should not donate organs after we die. What is your opinion?

After death, we should in fact not donate organs, but charge for them instead. Why give something so valuable away? Medicine charges a fortune for transplant operations, and somehow we are expected to give the most valuable part of that operation away for free out of the goodness of our hearts. We need to change this approach. Instead of carrying Organ Donor Cards, we should all possess Organ Sale Negotiation Cards, listing starting bid prices for each of our most valuable parts. Then let the free market and a qualified auctioneer decide who will get them and at what price, and our heirs will profit handsomely. With this approach, a family that can barely make mortgage payments on their home will be able to fix the roof and even add an addition onto their house after their loved one's organs have been sold to the highest bidder. Thus, the death of a loved one can have a positive long-term effect upon the surviving family.

THE CONSCIOUS BRAIN: OUR MOST OVERRATED ORGAN

While many feel that the conscious brain is the most exquisite creation in the universe, it is also responsible for most of the suffering in the world. Moreover, it does not make the crucial decisions in your life. For example, the conscious brain merely decides where to live, what to do for a living, whom to marry, and other minor issues. It is the unconscious brain that has the much more demanding job of regulating body temperature, heart rate, hormone levels, and blood pressure. Whether you live in Houston or Tampa, or marry Belinda or Frank, is not nearly as important as whether your thyroid hormone levels are too high or you have a 106-degree temperature with rapid heartbeat. Thus it is our unconscious, and not conscious, brain that plays the more significant role in our lives and possesses the greater intelligence.

YOU ARE NOT YOUR IDENTITY

Many people define themselves by their identity. This is a mistake. They believe they are either their job, their accomplishments, or their possessions. You are none of these things. Your true nature is separate from all of these so-called accomplishments. Buddhism teaches us there is nothing to attain. What you truly are cannot be affected by anything that you do. Our identity is nothing that we can possess or hold in our hands, but is only something we can experience when we remove all of these so-called "definitions."

Very often we are too attached to our possessions as definitions of ourselves. This problem reminds me of the cartoon character Elmer Fudd. After a car accident where he hit his head, he sat up in his hospital bed and said over and over again, "My name is Elmer J. Fudd. I own a mansion and a yacht." These thoughts were how he defined himself, the only link he had left to his ego-based reality. The car accident had enlightened him by emptying his mind, and yet he was determined to desperately hold on to this last shred of ego definition. The more frantically we try to hold on to these ideas, the more difficult it becomes because we know our "identity" runs deeper. Our true nature is calling out to us and we ignore it or even run from it.

These possessions and ideas are indeed such a small part of ourselves that to stay there is to guarantee misery. That is why *misery* and *miser* come from the same root word, meaning "wretched."

They used to name hospitals after charitable and religious organizations. Not anymore—they are now run by accountants and MBAs. I recently visited a friend at Our Lady of the Bottom Line Hospital in Baltimore. He was told by some thugs from the hospital accounting office to pay up right away, or things might get worse. He came in to heal a broken leg, but they told him that if he didn't pay up soon, he'd have a broken arm.

My friend, whom we'll call Gil, because that's his name, had a life-threatening illness on top of that. But he was most concerned about a valuable silver pendant that he had left overnight on the table, and which was now missing. Gil's identity was strongly connected to this possession. He was convinced that one of the nursing staff had taken it, and found this more upsetting than his weakening state of health. I asked him to stop panicking and listen to his breathing, so that he might realize that the missing pendant was not as important as attaining a sense of awareness about his life. He couldn't get the pendant off his mind, and spoke constantly about how he wanted to give it to his eldest son as his father had given it to him on his deathbed. Never mind that I had taken it from him in order to teach him a spiritual lesson: the point was that it was all he could think about at a time when more important thoughts about human existence should have been filling his consciousness. The universe, whether through my intervention or by its own will, always supplies us with the experiences we need in order to grow. In the end, my taking of the pendant helped my friend see things the way they should be seen. Thus, if there is anything I "stole" from him, it was an unwanted part of his consciousness.

Later that week, Gil passed away. I mourned his passing, and then sold his pendant for a large sum, much more than I thought it was worth. I then spent the money the way I knew Gil would have wanted it spent: frivolously, on meaningless things and activities.

There were two spiritual lessons in this journey for me. First, reflecting on the pendant and its enormous value, I realized that what we possess is often worth far more than we know. Second, I spent all the money on having fun and yet empty experiences for myself. In the end, they all meant nothing. I felt relieved that I had prevented my friend from having to go on this vacant journey. I had learned a lot about the value of objects, and also how meaningless life can be in the end if we merely focus on material or sensual pleasures, such as exquisite food and wine and expensive day cruises around Manhattan. It all goes to show that when we help friends in a time of need to grow, we grow, too.

Two Weeks

Even worse than aligning your identity with your possessions is when you assume someone else's identity. Someone recently did this to me, and stole my identity. He ran up large bills on my credit cards by eating at pricey restaurants, purchasing expensive items at appliance stores, and going on exotic vacations. After one month, however, he called to ask if he could give me my identity back. He said my relatives were calling him, asking him to participate in a variety of social obligations. He also told me an ex-girlfriend of mine from long ago was bothering him. They were all making undue demands on his time, which he felt were an unfair invasion of his space. He agreed to pay off my credit card bills with interest and pay me an additional fee if I would go back to assuming my identity. We struck a deal, and he is now happy once again.

Two Weeks

What Is Meditation?

Whatever you are doing, you are meditating on it.
—Master Lohan

Master Lohan, in the brief time I knew him, transferred to me much of his knowledge about meditation. I asked him many questions during our time together, and what I remember from those discussions I will try to share here.

Meditation, Master Lohan said, is simply turning the brain off by sitting quietly. At first the mind may be busy, but after a while, like a spinning top with no one there to continue to spin it, the mind will come to a stop.

The comedian Robert Klein once said that after taking a speed-reading course, he learned how to read so fast that he could no longer read his name. It went by too quickly. This is our mind's relationship with the world. We have had to speed it up to learn our mind-centered jobs, and now we must slow it down again in order to truly experience the world around us.

Our minds get wound up like extension cords on phones, back in the days before everything went cordless. In order to unravel the twisted cord, you let the phone dangle and spin out. This is what meditation is: letting your mind do nothing but "unspin" so it can become disentangled from all the thoughts that have been holding it back for years and twisting it out of shape.

Many seek this unspinning sensation via alcohol, sensual pleasures, skydiving, or arguing followed by lovemaking, but these often merely distract or numb the psyche. Meditation makes our awareness more alive while also giving us the good news that nothing is really going on. Our mind is a drama queen. It wants to say that things are happening when they are not. Meditation is a reality check that says, no, nothing is really going on.

WHAT IS THE SOURCE OF ALL MISERY?

The Buddha said that the source of all misery is desire. Yet, in middle-class America, who makes us want things? Who places the desires and expectations in our heads? Our parents. They say we must go to college, graduate with excellent grades, then go to Yale Law School, buy the right house, marry the right person, "make them proud," and so on. Thus, they lodge themselves in our consciousness in such a way that we cannot differentiate their goals for us from our own desires. So, in America, the source of all misery, the Buddha would likely agree, is our parents.

USING THE POWER OF TWO WEEKS TO AVOID YOUR PARENTS

When your parents call, or ask you to come over, tell them you will get back to them in two weeks. Then say you forgot. Do this indefinitely. Through this method, you can lead yourself to a greater sense of peace and happiness. Soon, you will discover all of the things you did merely to make your parents happy, and stop doing them. You will get in touch with your true nature and realize that your grades in school don't matter to you. How much you are saving each year is of little interest as well. You'll see that when, and if, you get married is not that important. A deep bliss will begin to blossom in you, one you will recognize was always there. You just had to create the space for it to exist and listen to it.

AMERICA HAS BORDERLINE PERSONALITY DISORDER

The greatest threat to the mental health of America is mental illness. As someone once said, "A family is a dictatorship ruled by its sickest member." In the international scene, the world is a dictatorship ruled by its sickest member. And that would be us, America. That is because we, as a nation, have borderline personality disorder.

America does not respect or even recognize the boundaries of other countries. To us, these boundaries are nonexistent. This is one of the salient features of borderline personality disorder. If we put Americans in any country, that country becomes ours in our consciousness at that moment, and we lose the awareness that it might at one point have belonged to itself.

America views the very existence of other countries as a threat, just as borderlines view the existence of independent, happy people as threatening. Therefore, we like to invade other nations and make sure that our troops are in as many countries as possible. Only then does a borderline nation like America feel safe.

Other symptoms of borderline personality disorder that America exhibits include:
- a pattern of instability and irrational impulsivity in relationships
- paranoid ideation about the presence of nonexistent threats
- a pattern of unstable and intense fluctuation between extremes of idealization and devaluation

- chronic feelings of emptiness that must be filled with some sort of self-created drama
- inappropriate, intense anger or difficulty controlling anger and aggression

The treatment for America's borderline personality disorder will not be easy, and will involve many years of therapy. Getting the Pentagon on the couch won't be easy. We will need an extremely large armory filled with recliners, and an army of therapists. But the job must be done.

Or, like true borderlines, we may just wish to continue to deny the problem exists.

Two Weeks

Religion in America

Better to fail going in the right direction than succeed going in the wrong one. –Master Lohan

In order to understand America, we need to understand her religions. Let's look at the six most important religions in America: Abs, News, Lawn, Golf, Milk, and Flu Shots.

ABS

Abs, short for "abdominals," is now the largest religion in America. Abs followers believe that if you have strong and visible abdominal muscles, everything else in your life will go well. One third of all magazines are devoted to this faith. It is the simplest of all religions, requiring only a low-calorie diet and three hours in the gym every day.

NEWS

The second largest religion in America is News. This group uses anxiety as a source of peace. They believe that we need to be deeply concerned about at least twelve things per day that have nothing to do with us in order to feel any kind of serenity. Otherwise, they believe we have not truly experienced the day. This religion features "Newscasters" who distribute News freely over a range of media in order to "reel in" new believers while also maintaining old ones. Newscasters are often charismatic and attractive people, which further helps them convince us of the significance of News. Their believers assert that we must live vicariously through as many strangers as possible for as much of our lives as we can. Some believers in this sect watch news services up to twelve hours a day in order to stay abreast of everything that doesn't directly affect them. It is only when they are sufficiently filled with worry from all the News they have absorbed and filled with the feeling that they have not missed anything that they are relaxed enough to go to sleep.

LAWN

Lawn is the religion that makes my line of work possible. Lawn believers feel that no matter the state of relations in their families, or the quality of their health, or conditions in the world at large, as long as their lawn is green and healthy, all is well in their lives. Although lack of communication among those close to them is not something they like, weeds in the lawn lead them to a state of panic. Even if toxic pesticides must be used to maintain order in such a lawn, no matter: Lawn believers are convinced that any means are justified to achieve a smooth, green lawn. Without it they are lost. Lawn followers also usually discriminate strongly against those who do not believe in the postulates of Lawn. They will say nasty things about them behind their backs. The village of Skokie, Illinois forces lawn owners to mow their lawns on a daily basis, and should they fail to do so, the city will cut it for them and send the homeowner a hefty bill. The Skokie village council is currently considering a hedge trimming ordinance which may well go into effect early next year.

GOLF

Scholars once believed that Golf was an ancient rite invented by South Sea Islanders. These primitive people believed in a hungry god who lived in the mountains and who could only be placated if eighteen holes were drilled all over the island and white balls were placed in each of these sacred indentations in ceremonial succession. These holes had to be connected by smooth, grass-covered fields tended to by a special caste of workers. The area near the hole had to have the smoothest, flattest grass available, maintained by these sacred grass keepers, and be surrounded by ceremonial pits of sand to ward off the evil spirits who wanted to contaminate the rituals that transpired there. And the balls could not merely be placed in the holes—they had to land there by first being struck from a great distance with sacred sticks fashioned from the bones of whales. Shamans watched the entire event to make sure that all ceremonial rules were maintained. The natives followed the proceedings around the island in silent awe, punctuated with occasional bursts of hysterical applause when things were done well. All of this was necessary to keep the local volcano from erupting and burying the entire island and its inhabitants in molten lava.

We know today, however, that this is not true. Golf was invented in Scotland in the fifteenth century. Regardless of its true origins, however, Golf is tied deeply to many a golfer's spirituality. The only downside of Golf is that it has kept life forms from other planets from landing on Earth. NASA scientists have documented that when flying saucers hover above a golf course and see sand traps—evidence that humans make things harder for themselves on purpose—they turn around and leave.

MILK

Milk is a small and obscure religion that exists in coastal

regions of the southern and eastern United States. The origin of this religion is not clear, but what we do know is that people in these regions who follow this creed use milk to ward off hurricanes. At times I, too, have been a follower of Milk. I don't drink it, am somewhat allergic to it, but when there is a hurricane approaching, I follow the masses to the supermarket and purchase it. I see everyone doing it and hear that it might run out soon, so I buy a gallon. At first I asked my fellow believers at the supermarket if I need to pour milk over my front door, pour it down every drain in my house before the hurricane comes, or perform some other ritual with it. No, they said, merely having it is enough. Does it need to be in the center of the fridge, alone? I asked. No, just having it in the fridge is enough. The key is to make sure that the expiration date of the milk is later than the predicted landfall of the hurricane.

As the hurricane passes over, I feel comforted knowing the milk is there, even as the lights flicker and the rain and wind whip against the windows. I see tree branches and road signs fly by, but I remain calm. I put myself at ease by walking into the kitchen, and, amid the sounds of devastation, meditating on the sight of the miraculous white liquid in the fridge. The power may go off. Trees may fall. The milk itself may then begin to warm. But it stands fast. This milk doesn't run. Then, when the hurricane has passed, I pour it down the drain. As I do so, I say a prayer of gratitude to the cows who provided it, the grass upon which they fed, the megadoses of antibiotics fed to them, the automated machines which yanked the milk out of them, and to our natural world as a whole, which so magically provides protection from every form of destruction it creates.

FLU SHOTS

Flu Shots is another very unusual religion that began here in America. Like many of our other home-grown faiths, it has already spread over many parts of the world. Flu Shots only protect against one or two strains of the influenza virus, yet over three hundred strains of flu abound each year, hoping to take root in our weakened immune systems. Flu Shots, then, are nothing more than a Maginot Line against the blitzkrieg of viruses to which we are exposed each and every winter. Nonetheless, millions of Americans line up dutifully to receive these questionable injections which, while providing little benefit, offer a wide range of side effects. Why do we believe in Flu Shots? No one is certain. The ritual itself seems to create a closeness among family members. Sons and daughters will contact parents and ask, "Have you had your shot?" Never mind the lack of evidence: those who believe in Flu Shots have a strong faith that cannot be shaken, and the Churches of the Flu Shot are filled every fall and winter with lines of countless loyal followers taking their yearly communion of this sacred mixture.

NOT BOTHERING ANYONE

One of the quietest, most wonderful and most underappreciated religions in America is known as the Church of Not Bothering Anyone. It is a church that never meets. Members politely go about their business each day in their various roles throughout society.

Followers of this church do their jobs quietly and pleasantly, and then go home. They do not create problems for anyone else. They are peaceful and kind to people and animals alike. This sect is also against invading other countries, especially if it involves disturbing or killing anyone or displacing anyone from their homes. To them, the perfect existence is a pleasant workday, going home to eat dinner, and looking back at the day and realizing they did not trouble a single person. They call this "Nirvana." My grandfather belonged to the Church of Not Bothering Anyone, and it was from him that I learned of this simple faith.

IS THE POWER OF TWO WEEKS A RELIGION?

Yes. It had its beginnings at the very start of human history. We know that ancient civilizations embraced *The Power of Two Weeks from Now*. They knew that two weeks was a magical period of time that needed to be respected. It was just far enough into the future to seem as though it would never arrive, yet close enough to be comprehensible.

Cave paintings demonstrate the power of two weeks clearly. When confronted with bad weather, early cave artwork shows the phrase:

Rain, rain, go away, never come back

Unfortunately, these civilizations perished due to drought.

Ten thousand years later, the following phrase was found in cave paintings in the south of France:

Rain, rain, go away, come back a week from Tuesday

For such an enormous advance to occur in so short a period of time shocked paleontologists, yet it did not last. The shaman or prognosticator who wrote this phrase was beheaded, because apparently there was a very important event planned for a week from Tuesday. This phrase was soon forgotten and never seen again.

Then, only two thousand years later, the following phrase appeared in a cave in northern Italy:

Rain, rain, go away, come again another day

Scientists on the scene of this discovery were again deeply

impressed by so great an advance in so short a period. They suggested that the Neolithic symbol used in the cave painting to signify "another day" most likely means "two weeks" in our modern calendars. Thus we see the amazing origin of human denial. Ancient peoples long ago appreciated the power of ambiguity and the need to push things off into the future in order to be happy. In this cave painting, we see the first sign of delaying and ignoring something until some unknown point in the future as a way to create peace and joy. Serenity derived from denial entered human consciousness for the first time. The idea of the power of two weeks was born.

Losing the Moon

If our love is only a will to possess, it is not love.
—Thich Nhat Hanh

I **headed out to Las Vegas** to spend more time with Master Lohan. I needed to see him again and try to learn more from him in person. I had read all his books, but that was not enough. I needed to be with him. Master Lohan said he would be happy to take time off from work at the car dealership and spend a few days with me.

He said that we should spend the four days of my visit camping in Red Rocks Park, seventeen miles from Las Vegas. It's funny—Kelly always wanted me to go camping. I never went, telling her I got enough nature at work everyday. Maybe we should have gone camping together at least once, instead of her always going with Cleo. Maybe that would have helped things.

We hiked all day, and camped at night. I found I really liked sleeping on the ground. Red Rocks Park is amazingly beautiful. The weather was perfect. We had clear skies every night. Each evening we looked up at the moon, which was nearly full the first night I got there. Each time Master Lohan would ask me the same question.

"What is the moon?" he said.

"I don't know," I said. "A part of the earth that broke away a long time ago?"

He shook his head no.

"A wandering planet that just started orbiting the earth millions of years ago?"

He shook his head no again.

He asked me again on the second night.

"What is the moon?"

"A place we go and visit now and then?" I said.

Again no.

Finally, on the third night, I answered.

"It's Kelly," I said.

"Yes," he said. "Why?"

"Because ... Kelly loves space. The moon has a lot of space around it."

"Yes," he said. "The moon cannot be happy unless it has a lot of space."

We stood there in silence. I thought about Kelly, and how glad she was whenever she had come back from one of her weekend retreats. The craters on the moon looked happy, like

Kelly's smile.

"The moon is also joyful," he said, "because no one is walking on her. And no one is telling her to what to feel. She can have any mood she likes any time, and no one argues with her."

I thought about Kelly, and how she had a different mood for each day—sometimes each moment—sometimes happy, sometimes sad, sometimes smiling, yet still dark like a crescent moon, other times covered with clouds so I could not see what was going on underneath.

"What else do you notice about the moon?" Master Lohan asked.

"You can't see the stars as well when the moon is full."

"Right," he said. "And who would want to? That would be greedy. The moon has all the beauty you need. Why would you want to look elsewhere?"

"I don't," I said.

He held out a box of ginger candies to me.

"Want one?" he asked.

"Sure," I said, reaching for one. He pulled the box away.

"Then you should've gotten some before we left." He ate the last one. "You need to plan ahead more, Kincaid."

We started to get into our sleeping bags and kept looking up at the moon. I listened to the wild animals in the distance and wondered if they would come up to us as we slept. All the food was in my car, so there was nothing they could want here. I realized we would probably be fine.

"Who owns the moon?" Master Lohan asked, getting into his sleeping bag.

"No one," I said.

"Right. And even if someone is close to the moon, or even marries the moon, he doesn't own it. It still needs lots of space around it to be happy. Understand?"

"Yes," I said. "But Master Lohan, is Kelly ever coming back?"

"Is the moon ever coming back?" he said.

I thought for a moment.

"So, she's not," I said.

"No."

"Why not?"

"She's more evolved than you."

"How do you know?" I asked. "You've never met her."

"I know you," he said, and fell asleep.

The following night, I had a midnight flight back east. Master Lohan insisted on driving me to the airport in the brand-new Toyota I had rented. He said he wanted to see how it handled the road.

"Smooth," he said. "Lighter than a Buick. I wonder what it would take to tip this Camry over."

We calmly rolled down the Strip around 10:30 p.m., and the moon was already high in the sky. The crowds were walking up and down the street. Master Lohan jerked his head around and looked at the moon as though he had never seen it before.

"What in the world is that?" he asked.

"The moon," I said.

"The moon? How long has it been following us?"

"I don't know—since we left Red Rocks."

"OK. Hold on."

He made a sharp turn off the Strip and we drove way too fast on a road behind the hotels. I was worried a cop would pull us over for speeding and I would miss the flight. I saw the moon flash momentarily between each hotel.

"Still there?" he asked, passing cars aggressively.

"Yeah, I guess," I said.

He made a sharp turn into the parking lot behind Caesar's Palace, practically tipping the car over and throwing me out of the window. He came to a sudden stop. We waited there a while. I caught my breath.

"Count down from ten," he said.

"Why?" I said.

"Just count."

I counted down slowly, and before I'd gotten to one, he screeched out, and we were almost hit by a cab filled with tourists he pulled in front of. Master Lohan then wove in and out of traffic going down the Strip, and kept up this crazy driving until we reached the outskirts of town. He then drove down a series of dirt roads, making sharp turns, and kicking up a lot of dust. We hid in parking lots behind buildings, then pulled out and, seeing the moon still there, started this mad cat-and-mouse game all over again. It went on for some time.

"Can't lose it," he said. "But I'm trying. She's fierce."

"But—" I tried to say something, but he was in his own world. I just held on for dear life and waited for the ride to end as we made one wild loop all around the edge of Las Vegas.

Before I knew it, we were at the curb of the airport. I was happy to walk on solid ground again. He helped me out with my bags, and told me he would return the Toyota, which was now covered in red Nevada dust. He seemed to have calmed down. I hardly recognized him. Was this the same serene man I had just camped with for three days?

"I guess you can't lose the moon," he said.

"Guess not," I said.

"You can try, but it won't work."

We got out of the car, shook hands, and said good-bye. I realized I was still scared and shaking from the dangerous drive. I leaned against the car to steady myself. I took a deep breath and just looked at the moon one more time.

"You know, Master Lohan, sometimes I think that when I get to the end of my life I'll look back and say, wow, I survived it. I mean, that doesn't make any sense, does it? To feel like you survived it, even though you're at the end. Know what I mean?"

"Sure, Kincaid."

I grabbed my bags and got ready to walk into the terminal.

"Kincaid, one more thing."

"Yeah?"

"I love you." He pulled me close and gave me a hug. I didn't know what to say.

"And so does a certain someone traveling around Mexico, whether or not you ever see her again. Know what I mean?"

"Sure, yes," I said. "I mean, I'm glad you love me."

"Yes," he said, getting back into the car. "But don't take it personally. I love everybody. Good-bye."

"Good-bye."

More Questions About *The Power of Two Weeks from Now*

Happy people are those who do things they don't like every day. –Master Lohan

The preacher at our church in Little Rock says that rap music is God's punishment for the entertainment industry's not fully promoting Perry Como during the height of his career. Is this true? Yes.

I owe back rent. Can Buddhism and The Power of Two Weeks help me?
 Yes. I had often tried to convince Mr. Leland that I am not the same person from moment to moment, so I shouldn't have to pay rent for someone who is no longer me. He then stood next to me for a few moments and said, "You're still the same person, and you still owe me six months' rent," so it didn't work. Then I embraced the power of two weeks, and

have agreed that I am the same person moment to moment, but that I need two more weeks to pay. This has been more successful, and I have stretched two-week extensions on my rent to now span months.

Do you envision the day when Buddhism makes it into professional sports, and a receiver scores a touchdown and then assumes the lotus position to acknowledge that the touchdown was really an illusion?
That day is coming soon.

How long does milk last past its expiration date?
Four and a half days at 45 degrees Fahrenheit.

How did the Boston Red Sox win the World Series twice within a period of a few years after failing to do so for over eight decades?
After their World Series victory in 2004, the consciousness of the fans of Boston and its players changed. It then became clear that victory was possible, and that being a Boston Red Sox fan was no longer a Puritan duty of self-flagellating disappointment. Pleasure, something completely unknown in New England since the 1620s, reappeared. Once this consciousness took root in the six states where Red Sox fans are most numerous, this consciousness spread. They began rediscovering simple pleasures such as walking in the park and enjoying food. People in Massachusetts began "smiling"

MORE QUESTIONS ABOUT *THE POWER OF TWO WEEKS FROM NOW*

again after someone passed out a pamphlet in downtown Boston on how to do it. Long-married couples began holding hands. Fathers who had warned sons not to open businesses now encouraged them to do so. The air of possibility and happiness began to return to New England. Everyone seemed to come back to life.

At the same time, the Red Sox players developed a consciousness known as "swagger." This is the belief that you are a talented player who will level the competition. These two collisions of consciousness then led to another championship victory three years later. This consciousness now seems firmly rooted in both the fans and the players, showing that more championship victories may lie in the near future.

Did evolution occur?
If it did, that would mean there had to be a moment in history when a fish walked out of the water. To test this theory, I sat for two weeks staring at the beach along the New Jersey coastline. I did not see a single fish walk out. Scientists say it took millions of years for so bold a fish to materialize. But, we know from the rules of common etiquette that if a fish does not walk out of the ocean in two weeks, he is not going to walk out at all. Thus, *The Power of Two Weeks from Now* disproves evolution and also saves us from having to sit on the beach for millions of years waiting for a fish to walk out, or even worse, earn a Ph.D. in evolutionary biology.

What is a koan?
A contradictory phrase one meditates upon to open up one's mind.

Why are they made up?
The goal is to make sense of it, and by doing so, attain enlightenment, or at least open your consciousness to a wider sense of awareness.

Can you give me an example of a koan?
My spiritual teacher, Master Lohan, gave me this koan when I first came to study with him: How is it possible to be thirsty and need to take a leak at the same time? I knew at once what he was getting at: how can you love and need something, and yet want to expel it? You want to bring it toward you, and yet at the same time you want to discard it. How, then, can you be in a love-hate relationship with anything? This koan is essentially about relationships.

I sat and meditated on it for two weeks and then realized the answer: the urinary system is separate from the thirst mechanism. That is all you need to know about relationships.

More koans:
- If a Hollywood star is shallow, why is she always invited back to Letterman?
- Can a Hummer park in a space made for a compact car?
- If a state bird becomes extinct, does its senator care?

Is an oxymoron the same as a koan?
An oxymoron is simply a contradictory pair of words. Examples include *rap music* and *compassionate conservatism*.

How can we improve the quality of street performers in our city?
Master Lohan once said regarding street performers: "If you don't like the performance, and if they are causing you suffering, take some money out of their box. This practice instantly improves the quality of street performers anywhere it is implemented."

Is there a way to return played-out celebrities to the obscurity from whence they emanated?
Master Lohan says that the notoriety of each well-known person should be revoked every five years, and that he or she must do something remarkable all over again to regain their fame and place in the public consciousness.

Can rocks undergo transformation and thus increase their power over us?
Yes. When raw diamonds are brought into the Diamond District in New York City, they are valuable, but not as valuable as they will be when cut by a master diamond cutter and mounted on a ring. Then, the rock becomes of such import that a man who looks at it on his wife's finger forgets many of the ideas he once had regarding various forms of

social interaction. Initially the rock sat in a cave, minding its own business, never wanting to influence anyone's social life. Then, it was taken out under dangerous and oppressive working conditions, shipped a great distance, marked up exponentially in price, and was then given the power to make a man limit certain hormonal desires. By taking so much of a man's income, the rock also decreases the social opportunities a man has. So, not only is the rock transformed, but it transforms those around it as well.

When do you recommend fertilizing a lawn?
At least twice a year, but sometimes up to four or five times. It depends on your climate and what kind of grass you have. The key is to apply fertilizer only when the grass is growing, otherwise you'll feed the weeds instead.

Two Weeks

Solving the World's Problems with Denial

Those are my principles, and if you don't like them…well, I have others. —Groucho Marx

INSPIRATION

A lot of people are looking for inspiration to solve the world's problems: global warming, pollution, hunger, and overpopulation. First we must realize where these problems originate—the need to do things now, to understand things immediately, and to solve problems in this very moment. If they had actualized *The Power of Two Weeks from Now*, and put off thinking, eating, creating, building, lovemaking, and the need to acquire money or political power, less would have been done. Fewer babies would have been born. This would mean more food for all, less fossil fuel consumption, and a cooler planet. Many of the world's problems stem from this perceived "need to solve problems."

MOTIVATION

It is, therefore, motivation that needs eliminating. It is the denial of the existence of problems that *The Power of Two Weeks from Now* seeks to cultivate. We seek to eliminate motivation, inspiration, and similar "core causes" of more advanced problems that these initial solutions can cause. By doing so, many of the world's greatest challenges can be eliminated.

For example, many people may ask you what you think of the strife in the Middle East. You may say that you do not care and have no interest in the topic. They reply, aghast and indignant: "You must care!" Yet this caring is part of the problem. Tell them that if everyone were as apathetic as you, there would be no problems in the Middle East. Yours is the example of the future.

Master Lohan, who is very concerned about world peace, sought to gather and encourage the emigration of the most apathetic citizens from the United States to the Middle East in order to bring about peace there. However, by the time they all got to the airport, they decided they didn't really care enough to go. It was the solution that nearly happened. Had they gone, Master Lohan might have won the Nobel Peace Prize for his brilliant work.

GOVERNMENT INEFFICIENCY

What is wrong with our government? How do we solve its problems? Perhaps you may be saying, "Who cares?" But it's your money they're spending. This is an important question.

I was standing in line at a post office pondering this very issue, and it took so long for the line to move that we each stood there for about an hour before reaching the window. We all bonded in such a way during this time together that we felt we should have a reunion. We exchanged phone numbers and agreed to meet in a year to commemorate our experience together. When we met, we broke into discussion groups to try to discover the best way to prevent the needlessly slow-moving line we had experienced. We did not find any solutions, but many warm and deep friendships have come about as a result of our continued contact.

HOW DO WE SOLVE WORLD HUNGER?

It is a well-known fact that humans can live for two weeks without food. This is true as long as people are given water, a place to stay, adequate clothing, and plenty of snack foods. Snack foods, according to women, are not "regular" foods. Thus, without eating regular food, and by invoking *The Power of Two Weeks from Now*, hunger could be forestalled indefinitely. Millions of lives could be saved.

ALCOHOLISM

Alcoholism is a major problem in America—at least for those who can't control their drinking. It is estimated that one in ten Americans has a drinking problem. The cost to society of this disease, beyond the ruined families and damaged children, is staggering. The overall pricetag to America for this disease is well over sixty billion dollars a year.

In order to understand this problem, for six months I attended both Alcoholics Anonymous and Al-Anon meetings regularly, the latter support group being for relatives, loved ones, formerly loved ones, or anyone else affected by alcoholics and their paths of destruction. After attending these meetings, I realized that in both cases the inmates are running the asylum. Yes, some alcoholics are able to stop drinking, but an onerously long series of steps is needed to get the job done: twelve. In addition, there are no degreed professionals in charge.

Of the two groups, the recovering alcoholics were more interesting than the Al-Anon people. The recovering alcoholics had devil-may-care attitudes and interesting war stories to tell. Those in Al-Anon were sheepish types who for some reason continued to put up with these bozos when they should have moved on with their lives a long time ago.

After much thought, I came up with my own four-step system to replace the needlessly lengthy twelve-step system:

1. Drink only one or two drinks per day, unless it is a special occasion.
2. See a therapist twice a month.
3. Meditate.
4. Give me a dollar.

This system would attract a great many more people, because it allows one to two drinks per day, while the twelve-step approach makes you stop completely. The Buddhist "middle way" suggests that one or two might be fine. Secondly, four steps are easier than twelve. None of the active alcoholics I have talked to on the street or in abandoned buildings ever knows the twelve steps. That's poor marketing for you. And giving me a dollar for each participant at each meeting will allow me to build a large superstructure of management above all these meetings that will make them less efficient. Twelve-step meetings as conducted now run smoothly and seem to help almost everyone there, fostering a kind of egalitarianism that threatens other large organizations in America. They do not suffer from any good old American bureaucratic inefficiency, and that is what makes them seem so unpatriotic. They work too well.

Everyone derives some benefit. This must change if they are truly to go mainstream.

APPRECIATING OUR NATURAL WORLD

There was a pope in the 20th century who said that he liked the simple people best, meaning the peasants who lived in the countryside. At first I thought this was because he knew he could fool them more easily. But then I realized that it was because the closer we are to nature, the more we are likely to have an appreciation of the natural world, an inner beauty, and an open-heartedness that today is rare. Maybe that's what the pope liked about simple people. They were beautiful on the inside, embodied the wonder of the universe around them, and were also less likely to ask the tough questions.

The average American today has lost that sense of wonder about our natural world. Consider America and her forty-eight contiguous states. See how magically they fit together, as if through some divine design. Any child who has done a puzzle of the states knows how seamlessly they snap together, and yet adults, with our busy minds, have forgotten this and lost the sense of awe we once had about our natural world. Thus, it often takes the mind of a child to see the miracle of creation right before us.

Perhaps it is because of this disconnection from what is around us that we have neglected our impact on the natural world, and due to that, the earth is getting warmer. Though the rise in temperatures is generally blamed on greenhouse gases, or solar activity, or both, the earth may just be getting mad from neglect, getting hotter as it gets angrier.

Yet, no matter the cause of global warming, one thing is clear: we must deny it.

Two Weeks

The Importance of Denying Global Warming

I am an evil giraffe, and I shall eat more leaves from this tree than perhaps I should, so that other giraffes may die. –Eddie Izzard

Global warming is easy to deny, because other than rising temperatures, there is no evidence that it is occurring. Unless you live near a glacier and watch it recede, or are on an island where the waters are rising and threatening to sink your way of life into the sea, no one really knows it is going on. Plus, it may be that someone is stealing the glaciers very slowly. No one has actually seen them get smaller in one sitting, so we can't be sure that melting is occurring. Plus, the glaciers could be hiding. They could be going underground. Maybe they are just becoming shy.

Another way to deny global warming is to change the way we measure temperature. We could recalibrate 30 degrees Celsius to represent what is now 40 degrees Celsius with the expression, "30 is the new 40." This will be easily accepted by the public. Thus, the earth will actually appear to cool suddenly, a great comfort to many populations worldwide. The hard part is to convince ice to form at the new temperatures, but the public relations industry may be able to fool it into doing so by setting up some clever campaigns in the polar regions.

However, the mounting science confirming global warming is getting harder than ever to cover up. The first thing we have to do is distract NASA scientist James Hansen, Ph.D., the leading researcher on global warming, from continuing to marshal the evidence that we have very little time to change our behavior in order to prevent catastrophic ice melts in this century. He keeps saying we must move away from coal and oil and other fossil fuels as energy sources. He clearly doesn't like people who sell coal and oil, and this is obviously nothing but a personal vendetta. His evidence, however, is annoyingly well documented. What can be done to silence his voice?

It is well known at NASA that Dr. Hansen likes caramel-covered popcorn. Perhaps the coal industry could send him a few tins every week to munch on while he's crunching the numbers. Tasty popcorn has been used to sway many a scientist and change undesirable findings. Maybe they could also include some high-quality root beer, which he also likes. It is also rumored that Dr. Hansen is a great fan of roller-coasters. Perhaps oil industry executives could arrange for him to have a lifetime pass to the world-class amusement park in Cedar Point, Ohio, so he could visit it as often as he likes. Maybe then he would stop being such a bother to the energy industries and go out and have some fun for a change.

WHY IT IS IMPORTANT TO CONTINUE TO DENY GLOBAL WARMING

Were we to accept the scientific facts that Dr. Hansen presents as "real," we would need to make wholesale changes in our economy, lifestyle, and energy sources. This could cause considerable suffering in the near term. And it is in the near term, as all economists and denial experts know, that we all live in, moment by moment. So, by denying Dr. Hansen's evidence, we can continue to enjoy life in the near term to the utmost and not feel compelled to lift a finger or change our lives.

The time is ripe to do nothing.

Let us also remember all the positive things about global warming:

- A shrinking U.S. land mass means higher real estate values and more togetherness as we all huddle together.
- The Weather Channel is now the most boring channel

on TV. Global warming will lead to chaotic and catastrophic weather worldwide, which will make it thrilling to watch every night.
- Melting ice caps will provide an ample supply of clean, fresh drinking water, which will be needed in countries such as India, when their glaciers vanish.
- Global warming will lead to a significant reduction in species worldwide, which will in turn make conservation efforts easier. The fewer species there are, the easier it will be to protect the remaining ones. Thus, as the number of species declines, our conservation efforts will paradoxically seem much more effective.
- Beaches will vanish. This is good news, for it will eliminate those long hot walks on the sand one had to endure to get to the waves. You'll soon be able to step right out of your hotel lobby into the ocean.
- Global warming is good news for Puerto Rico and other wannabe states. Puerto Rico has been shut out of statehood because there are already fifty stars on the flag, and America will never have a fifty-one star flag due to design problems. When Delaware submerges, Puerto Rico will be welcomed with open arms. Instead of going to a forty-nine star flag, the government would much rather sign up a new state.

The Iroquois Nation believes that every decision we make must be judged based on how it affects our descendants seven generations from now. The good news is that since we've done such a good job ignoring global warming, it is unlikely that there will be many people around seven generations from now, so we no longer have to concern ourselves with this complex and difficult question.

HOW TO DENY HUMANS CAUSE GLOBAL WARMING

While it may seem challenging to deny global warming, it is in fact easy. Here are some strategies:

- Find one scientist, radio talk-show host, or short-order cook who doubts the connection between human activity and global warming. Quote him or her extensively whenever the topic comes up. Even though hundreds of scientists believe in the link, one doubter is all you need to sleep at night.
- Say that as far as you're concerned, the temperature has not been rising.
- Say you don't go for all this "physics" stuff, and that aside from the time you fell out a window and broke your leg, you have never seen it applied in real life.

If that doesn't work, we should make light of global warming. Making fun of things is another way to avoid them. Here are some new state slogans for license plates, which have the additional benefit of helping us brace ourselves for what appears to be the inevitable:

> **Florida**
> **Keep All Your Ice, Antarctica!**

> **Maryland**
> **Getting Ready for New Borders**

> **Colorado**
> **It's Nice Not to Be Coastal**

> **Kansas**
> **Landlocked 'n Lovin' It**

Since so many state slogans argue over which state was the first to accomplish something, such as the Ohio and North Carolina dispute over the origins of flight, perhaps Delaware may want to get a jump on their claim:

> **Delaware**
> **First in Submersion**

SHOWING EARTHLY PRIDE

We should be proud of global warming. It was a tremendous accomplishment. The cab driver in Taipei, the combine operator in Saskatchewan, the woman in Russia turning on a light fed by a coal-fired plant, and the oil executive in Houston have all been working independently, but together have accomplished something extraordinary. No one person alone deserves the credit. When the earth is as hot as Venus, we can easily hire ourselves out and earn free transport to colder planets by putting this advertisement on our next deep-space probe:

Homo Sapiens:
We Warm Planets Better than Any Other Species

Your Planet:
Warmed in 200 Years or Your Money Back

See Our Sample Model: Earth
Western Spiral Arm of Milky Way Galaxy

Two Weeks

Our Ideas About the Past Are Based Solely on Memory

To err is human, to forget is ... something good, I don't remember what. –Master Lohan

Learning to forget is important. It is a large part of denial. If you can forget things as well as many of our leaders can, you, too can enter into a state of bliss and wear the ecstatic smile that so many people around Washington possess. They are totally in the moment, and have forgotten what they said just ten minutes ago. Forgetting and the joy it brings is not just for our elected officials. It is for us, too.

A leader in eliminating memory was former Attorney General Alberto Gonzalez. By using the simplest form of denial, he was able to completely stonewall an investigation by a House of Representatives committee regarding a rash of unwarranted firings of U.S. Attorneys. He showed us that anything can be denied easily by forgetting. By saying the following phrase over seventy times, he taught us how simple it is to deny. His nearly universal answer was:

"I do not recall."
or
"I do not recall that conversation."

When trouble is brewing around your house, and an investigation begins, imagine that you, too, are being investigated by a House committee as Alberto Gonzalez was. Suppose you were under oath from a congressional committee and were asked,

"Mr._____, do you recall that yesterday afternoon, while you were heading out to run errands, your wife asked you to buy lemons for a dessert she was making, and yet you returned home without them?"

Listen to your lawyer whisper sage advice into your ear, nod knowingly, and then lean into the microphone and say, with a grimace on your face,

"I do not recall."

Whether you do recall or not is not important. The answer is immediately respected, and does not allow for further questioning. Your wife will have no further recourse if you claim that you do not remember the incident. She may be upset, but you are off the hook. It is that easy to deny, and that powerful a tool.

I have a friend who is a Boston Red Sox fan and who is plagued by bad memories. Never mind the recent championships achieved by this resplendent team—whenever I mention the name "Bill Buckner," he doubles over in pain, a frothy white substance begins to emanate from his mouth, and he is bedridden for a few days. This stems from an unfortunate incident in 1986 when Mr. Buckner, while playing first base during a critical moment of a World Series game, performed a staggeringly evocative impersonation of a croquet hoop. While his choreography seemed effortless, it was the wrong time and place to pretend to be a piece of lawn sports equipment. This imitation allowed the other team to score, and the Red Sox eventually lost the game and the series.

Due to the frequent lack of appreciation Mr. Buckner experienced from his neighbors in the years following this dance move, he was eventually forced to leave the state of Massachusetts and move to Idaho. Out there, collective psychosis over poorly fielded baseballs does not occur. The latest reports suggest Mr. Buckner to be happy in his new surroundings.

If only my friend were to realize that this event is far in the past, and that the area of New England has subsequently enjoyed enough sports triumphs to more than make up for the occasional misplays that may have occurred within its geographical boundaries. I dream that one day my friend will embrace *The Power of Two Weeks from Now* and become aware that in a fair world, all baseball errors should be forgiven in two weeks. If human beings, no matter how talented, were not prone to errors, there would not be an error column on the scoreboard in every major league ballpark. Indeed, if we wished to celebrate our humanity more, we would encourage more errors in baseball, not fewer, and see that the creative contributions of people like Mr. Buckner should be celebrated for their uniquely human qualities.

Two Weeks

Even More Questions About *The Power of Two Weeks from Now*

~~~~~~~~~~

If you are not happy simply because you are alive, nothing else will make you happy. —MASTER LOHAN

Here are more questions about *The Power of Two Weeks from Now*, collected from my many conversations with fellow gardeners at Harry's Feed, Seed and Weed Store here in New Jersey.

I like to walk around inside my house naked, but my neighbors complain about it. Is there a solution?
The photons in your house technically belong to you, so your neighbors have no business stealing those photons by looking at what you are doing. All the same, try to wear something, or at least close the curtains.

If everyone would just realize that you are just like totally

channeling the truth and that it is coming from that great place beyond all of us and that we are all united in this upward and forward movement together and that this is like totally the spiritually correct thing and that we are all one, would like my Mom start taking her vitamins and my Dad finally talk to her more than twice a year, and my neighbor put his dog on a leash and be nice to my sister?
Sure.

Do you have any principles for managing money in these tough times, when so many on Wall Street are being deceptive?
Yes:
1. Choose the right mattress.
2. Sew the mattress completely after inserting money.
3. Don't smoke in bed.

This will yield the greatest financial safety of any plan I know. Other ways to improve our financial state and stimulate the economy:
- Lower the prime rate to minus three. That will really get the economy going.
- Give each American a printing press in their home to help supply any extra funds needed in case they can't pay their bills.
- One day per month, allow Monopoly money to be used as legal tender.

Some say that in order to achieve enlightenment we must abandon all sexual activity and dedicate ourselves to meditation, while others say that it's best to get married and then go meditate because then you don't get distracted by reproductive urges. Which is the correct answer?
Whatever works for you.

Our daughter is getting very interested in musical theater. Is there anything we can do?
Usually an intervention with the whole family works well. Make sure to do it soon. Show her graphic photos of the size of dressing rooms on cruise ships, and the pay stubs of people who work there. That often ends any interest quickly.

I have read that Jesus and Buddha basically taught the same thing. Is this true?
No. Jesus says that if we don't believe in him, we go to a place He calls hell, while Buddha says we will just be born once more to go through another life of some kind.

Can we just forget about that difference? I just like reading about the love stuff they both agree on.
OK, you can forget about that difference part.

Plus, I'm really uncomfortable with the concept of "hell." Why did you have to bring that up?
Every spiritual book has to bring up something undesirable.

OK—but please tell me you are not going to bring up things like hunger and social and economic inequalities and then suggest that some form of action is required on the part of the reader. I prefer books that promote my self-involved, narcissistic lifestyle and leave it at that without going into promoting an awareness of class differences and our need to rectify social and material injustices through everyday actions.

I promise I won't go there.

Two Weeks

Do real men cry?
No, but imaginary men in fiction do. It's about time real men caught up with them.

How will I know when I am enlightened?
When you are routinely given the best seat in any restaurant. A maître d' is the best judge of any person's character.

I want to become enlightened, but I want to be allowed to hate just one person. Can't I?
No. You have to love everybody.

That's not fair!
I didn't make up the rules.

Are there any absolute truths?
Maybe.

My son wants to score well on his high school exams. Should he study or sit around visualizing a good grade?
He should sit around visualizing the correct answers to the questions, which can be easily obtained on the Internet these days.

Is there a solution to overpopulation?
Master Lohan says that if only one generation were to utterly abstain from any form of intimacy, we could solve this problem permanently.

Do you remove leaves from gutters?
No, I am a lawn worker only. You want to look in the Yellow Pages for gutter-cleaning specialists.

Two Weeks

The Power of Two Weeks from Now in Relationships

Love is the only logic. –Master Lohan

UNDERSTANDING WHERE WE COME FROM

I have settled many a neighborly dispute with regard to the origin of leaves on a lawn by simply pointing out the trees these leaves came from. Such understanding of origins has prevented many a fistfight and helped me keep many a customer.

In order to love our significant other and our relatives fully, we must understand their origins as well—where they come from, and why they feel the way they do. The reason for most of the negative emotions between men and women stems from the fact that in the hundreds of thousands of years we spent in the African savannah, there were no houses or lawns to maintain. Nature and grazing animals did this automatically. The DNA of men is thus not coded to take care of these kinds of living arrangements. When a woman asks a man to fix up the house, or take care of the lawn, this goes against his genetics and dissonance arises within him. Also, the love of riding a lawn mower, even by men with small lawns, can be explained genetically. It replicates riding on the back of a wild, noisy animal that eats the grass beneath it, is potentially dangerous, and leaves man to a life of enjoyment and leisure.

Men are often accused of only having one thing on their minds. There was a time when this was valuable. For many thousands of years, the survival of the human race was in question. During the Black Death in the Middle Ages, the population of Europe declined significantly. At that time, the man who only had one thing on his mind was the hero. He was heralded as he walked down the street. "There he is," people would say, "the man with only one thing on his mind. Hail him!" and then applaud. But it was his very success that has reversed all of this.

Our genetics as men have not changed, but we have become the victims of our own success. We, who helped the species survive difficult times, are now criticized for the very ambitions that led to humanity inhabiting every corner of the planet.

Since the only thing men have had on their minds for the past few million years is maintaining the population on the planet, and we have completed our job, perhaps now it is time for us to leave the earth and let women run everything. I know many women eager to see the fulfillment of this plan.

So you are saying shallow relationships are best?
Yes. Deep ones demand too much from the other partner, whereas in shallow ones we seek our own enlightenment, not fulfillment from another person. I realized this when reading Master Lohan's *Staying Strangers: How Not Getting to Know Your Mate Keeps Things Fresh*. We must feel connected to the entire human race in order to feel emotionally and spiritually well. If you become overly connected to one person, it will make this nearly impossible. Therefore, promiscuity is an essential part of the spiritual path.

Two Weeks

MEN HAVE A SPECIAL NEED FOR THE POWER OF TWO WEEKS FROM NOW

Most relationship problems begin from the inherent dissonance between the modern demands put on men and our utterly different genetically determined roles. Since our traditional role was the hunter, and hunting today is rarely the source of our families' sustenance, we cannot expect men to want to do anything now but sit around. This is why men watch football. They are merely embracing their hunting nature by valuing the ability of a man to throw an object at high speed at a moving target running diagonally across a field.

The lion, another hunter of the savannahs from which we sprang, sleeps eighteen hours a day. We need to understand that men often have the same need to sleep and do nothing. Men are not from Mars. They are from a hundred thousand years ago. Women are not from Venus. They are from the present moment. We are separated not merely by two weeks, but by a hundred thousand years. Language was invented by women as a way of trying to bridge this gap, but to no avail. Women have evolved, and men haven't. We men made this choice consciously. Let's not try to hide this, but work through it, by realizing that giving men two weeks to accomplish anything that is asked of them is the modern way of bridging and accepting the hundred-thousand-year gap.

Evolution affected men and women differently. Men stopped evolving at a certain point, falling in love with the primal urges of their primitive brain. This was necessary for the survival of the species. Men thought about evolving, but realized that if they fully embraced the nobler aspects of the human soul, the scheming and manipulative behavior often needed to convince women to remove their clothing might get lost in the process and the species might die out. Thus, for the good of humankind, men have purposefully and sacrificially retained their primal and scheming nature. We did not want to. We had to do it for the good of all.

In spite of this, women continually try to civilize men. This has led to the "soft males" we see so often in modern society. In fact, today it is rare to see a male who is not "soft." While the human race continues to reproduce, this softening of males is of great danger to the long-term existence of the human species.

We must constantly create space for men to go to their darker side in healthy ways. When men wish to spend all weekend watching sporting events, either live or on television, and communicate only through various grunting sounds that indicate a need for more snack foods and traditional, fermented drinks, what they are trying to do is preserve their primal nature and the human race itself. We, as a culture, need to respect this behavior. Men are merely feeding and nurturing their primitive brain. They know the lawn needs mowing. They know the roof needs fixing. But they also know that if they do not affirm their manhood first, the future of human life on Earth may be at risk. We must respect men's alignment with these inner priorities and honor these selfish desires, however self-indulgent and primitive they may seem.

YOU ARE NOT YOUR WIFE

Many men have a consciousness that is overly connected to that of their spouse. When first invited to attend a sporting event or an innocuous card game, a married man will respond, "I gotta check with my wife first." By invoking *The Power of Two Weeks from Now*, you can help these men begin to realize that they are not, nor have they ever been, their wives in this sense.

There is something that happens to a man after he has been married for a few years. He becomes enslaved to a mindset where he actually thinks he is his wife, and that his needs and desires are no different than hers. He forgets that once, long ago, he enjoyed carefree afternoons playing cards, drinking beer, watching sporting events, and joking around with his friends. All these memories have gone now, and he actually thinks he enjoys fixing things around the house, mowing the lawn, or gardening. He has forgotten himself. For a moment, a thought may flit across his mind that he actually doesn't like doing these things, but it will vanish quickly when he hears her voice. What he does and does not like has become so melded with her preferences that he is no longer able to sense the long-lost, innermost desires of his heart.

This is a kind of consciousness that can be changed. I have seen many men wake up from this trance, and realize they are something separate—they are themselves. Their marriages have been more rewarding and enjoyable as a result. These men have found a renewed vigor, and it all began with *The Power of Two Weeks from Now*.

If you have become enlightened with *The Power of Two Weeks from Now*, you will want to help such a mentally enslaved friend. Start by suggesting he attend a party that occurs in two weeks at your home. Describe the party as one where no women are allowed, and where beer will be consumed directly from the bottle. Tell him that coasters will not be used. Mention that a range of unhealthy snacks, snacks that long ago may have fallen out of his consciousness, will be served. Also let it be known that these snacks may fall upon the carpet and that they will not be vacuumed up immediately. This will begin to wake him up, causing him to remember fond moments from his college days when he was comfortable and content in messy surroundings. Inform him that pizza will also be eaten, and directly out of the box, not on fine china. He will at once realize the absurdity of eating pizza on expensive Hungarian porcelain, as you continue to dislodge arbitrary rules regarding the ingestion of foods that have been placed deeply and subtly within his consciousness. Tell him to reserve the date. His wife is not likely to object as such an event seems harmless enough, and since it is two weeks away.

We have seen many such men achieve awakenings at parties such as these and return to their former selves. A moment comes when the man will hold up a bottle of beer and a fried corn chip and then look at a stain on the basement carpet that will never come out, and come to a deep realization. The man will remember a part of himself he long ago forgot existed. After such a realization, he often will remain in a speechless state for ten minutes or more, staring catatonically at the television set, experiencing a condition of unbridled joy and peace.

AVOIDING CONFRONTATION USING
THE POWER OF TWO WEEKS FROM NOW

Let's say you're out with your wife or girlfriend. She is getting confrontational, asking you if you have performed certain tasks, or if you think someone is thin or fat, or your overall opinion of certain friends' hairdos or social decorum. Invoke *The Power of Two Weeks from Now*. Let your mind wander and don't listen too closely—just enough to know when she's stopped talking. Maybe there is an upcoming sporting event you can think about. Then she'll say, "Are you listening to me?" Nod. But the true answer is no. You haven't been listening at all, and because you weren't listening, you avoided an argument and the relationship shall live to see another day. By ignoring her, you are showing that you really love her and care about the relationship.

USING THE GREAT SACREDNESS
TO AVOID YARD WORK

In Buddhism, there is a doctrine known as *The Great Sacredness*, which states that everything is perfect the way it is. If your wife notices that the near-complete defoliation of your trees has covered the grass in the backyard, she may ask you to remove these leaves. You may rightly point out that the backyard is perfect as it is even though it is covered with leaves, claiming the truth of *The Great Sacredness*. She may then say that she wants the yard to look as perfect as the neighbors', and point out that after they raked up their leaves their yard "looks more perfect than ours." The best solution may be to go ahead and rake the leaves so you don't miss any more of the game.

ATTENTION PROBLEMS IN SCHOOL

Very often, when children are not paying attention in school, it is due to the many wonderful, creative thoughts swirling about in their heads. The powers that be insist that such children be given medications to make them focus more on the lessons being taught. Instead, *The Great Sacredness* teaches us that each child is perfect as he/she is. Teachers should instead be given drugs to make them more interesting. This will remove the need to medicate any students, will not disturb the creative nature of young minds, and will lead to more interesting stories for children to tell their parents at the dinner table.

CRIMES OF PASSION

When you come home and find your spouse in the arms of someone else, the temptation is to get upset or even violent.

This is where *The Power of Two Weeks from Now* can play a helpful role. Other philosophies suggest that you count to ten. *The Power of Two Weeks from Now* recommends that you count to 1,209,600—the number of seconds in two weeks. In other words, leave at once, and take a two-week vacation on your own. This fling your spouse is involved in may last only two weeks. Then, using the power of denial, you can return home and both of you can pretend nothing happened, and avoid an expensive and stress-producing divorce.

TALKING CAN BE A PROBLEM

Ever since I had my great realization regarding denial and *The Power of Two Weeks from Now*, I am occasionally asked, when not working on yards, to offer advice to individuals and couples. When doing couples counseling, I often ask the couple if they have been on speaking terms during the last year. They usually say yes. Almost always something someone has said has caused a problem and brought the couple to me. Well, I say, putting two and two together, since talking has caused difficulties, let's try not talking. Not talking can be a great aid to a relationship. What I then suggest is: when either one of them arrives home from work, they not talk, but hold each other in their arms on the couch for twenty minutes. Then, they eat dinner in silence. They just look at each other and appreciate each other. Then, they go to bed. At daybreak, they have a nice morning kiss, then they share a silent breakfast together, and then it's off to work to begin the silent process all over again. On the weekend, there is no talking either. They can read together, go to a movie, take a walk, attend a play, but not converse. They continue this process for a year. What men and women usually discover is that they are often much more comfortable not talking to each other, and say they enjoy the nonverbal relationship enormously. Though the couple may not know the details of each other's lives during this period, they do develop a deeper appreciation of each other's presence. As they become strangers, they get to know each other more intimately, and their enjoyment of and interest in each other grows.

The lesson is straightforward. As Master Lohan says in his classic guide, *Women are from Pluto, Men are from the Asteroid Belt,* having a relationship can ruin a marriage. By simply removing the verbal, we can often allow a marriage to heal. The more distant you are from the one you love, the more you will enjoy each other and be glad you are alive. The goal is to give your partner as wide a berth as possible. You want to talk to them as infrequently as you can and not get so close that it ruins whatever idealized misconceptions you both had that attracted you to each other in the first place.

In the end, it may be that the ideal marriage occurs between two people who never meet.

GIVING THE OTHER PERSON SPACE

The Buddhist teacher and author Thich Nhat Hanh said that "true love is always the gift of more space." This is so true. Years ago, there was a woman I loved very much. I spent every moment I could with her. And yet this did not seem to make her happy. I felt at times she needed more space, for my love seemed to be crowding her. As I began to give her more space, I watched her begin to enjoy her life more. Eventually I gave her so much space that I completely lost touch with her. I have heard that today she is a very happy and fulfilled woman.

Two Weeks

Questions and Answers About Relationships

Be the source for all you seek. –Master Lohan

My *wife throws sharp items at me as I come in the front door from work each day. What can I do?*

Love her more. See where you're failing to open up your heart to her. Attend personal growth seminars to understand why your love energy is blocked. Her throwing things at you may be her attempt to help you open up these blocked heart pathways. Also, try the side door.

Sometimes she throws things out of the second floor window when I don't take out the garbage without being asked.

This hurling of objects from above is a sign that her emotions do not have a place to go. Give her passion a place to be met and felt. Consider a candlelight dinner, a massage, and then a romantic evening at home. Wait on her hand and foot until you discover what is wrong in your behavior that is causing her to act this way.

Is there a way to make intimate encounters today more meaningful, especially among those who view dating and relationships as passé and who engage in "hook-ups" and other forms of non-relationship-based sexual behavior?
Yes. We must bring back the old sexual mores.

But won't these just be ignored?
Yes—but that's just the point. Bring them back, and then ignore them. The problem today is that we don't even have something to ignore. That's how morals worked in the past. They were an unattainable ideal, and they motivated us to aim high before we went off and did something at odds with them. Parents and children could smile at each other at the dinner table, both believing such morals were being followed. The most important thing was that at least we had something to reach for in the first place. Today we don't even have that. America's greatest accomplishments—the invasion of Grenada, the *Police Academy* series, the MGM Grand, the development of low-maintenance sod—were built on the suppression of sex and the channeling of that energy into something else. By once again vilifying and suppressing our

sexual desires, followed by denying whatever it is we may end up doing, we can once again regain the moral greatness our culture once pretended it had.

My grandmother says that if you sing at the table, you will marry a crazy husband. Is this true?
Yes.

I met this wonderful girl who I spent every day with for two months. I really felt we were soul mates, but then she changed her hairstyle and now for some reason I have lost interest in her. Am I shallow?
No.

Why do men wear earrings?
So if one is found in the car, they can say, "Oh, that's mine."

Have black holes ever occurred on Earth?
Yes. They materialize as narcissists.

Does Master Lohan have any special rules for giving wedding gifts?
Master Lohan says wedding presents should not be given until a marriage has lasted at least ten years. The lure of presents coming in the future may be one of the most powerful ways to keep a couple working to maintain their relationship. While living without a toaster or fine china for

a decade can be hard, it is a small price to pay to keep the family going. Master Lohan says we can't reward people for a journey they say they are going on, but only when they have completed a good portion of the trip.

I have this recurring dream every night where my boyfriend and my mother are both standing on a tree stump under which they have buried my briefcase, which holds this big project I am doing at work. If I could only get the briefcase, I could get the promotion I want and be happy. What does this dream mean?
Sorry. This one is not clear to me.

I just met a girl who said she is a goddess and that I should worship her.
What is she like?

Loving, soulful, thoughtful, sultry, romantic—
Worship her.

My parents are annoying me. Even though I am happily married and the mother of two children, they want to involve themselves in every aspect of my life. What can I do?
I suggest running a tiny little experiment: ask your parents not to contact you for three years. Then, see if you seem slightly happier. If so, continue the experiment for another three years. If, after that time, you feel brighter in your moods

and more confident, try it for another three years. If after these nine years have past, you feel as though your life is under control and going in the right direction, you know you have done the right thing and should continue with this approach.

My wife, after fifteen years of marriage, has begun to be slightly negative about a few things. Last week, I met a young woman at work who is much more positive and upbeat about everything. She even sees rainy days as happy. I need to be around this kind of positive energy in order to grow spiritually. Can I divorce my wife and marry this younger, more positive woman so I can be in the best spiritual place for my own growth?

Yes, of course. Spiritual growth always comes before anything else.

Why are Canadian women happier than American women?

They know they will not run out of water as we are about to do here in the United States. This means they can take long showers indefinitely, which is a woman's favorite pastime.

Traveling with Master Lohan

The West must not only be seen to be believed, but it also must be believed to be seen.
—Native American saying

Master Lohan asked me to meet him in Las Vegas so we could drive cross-country together. He said it was an important thing for us to do, and that there were many things we needed to experience and see together.

We got into his 1970 Buick Electra 225 convertible, which was covered with bumper stickers—"It's Easier If I Go First," "I Believe in Life Before Death," "I'm Part of the Generation That Trashed the Planet," and "My Son Is Kept at Detention Daily at Rogers High."

"You have a son?" I asked him.

"No," he said, "should I?" He looked at the bumper stickers and smiled. "Used car."

We drove first to the Great Salt Lake in Utah, where he

made me float on my back in the water. I wondered if this was some kind of special initiation. There weren't many people around, but there were lots of flies. I was amazed how easy it was to float in the lake. This was because of all the salt in it, Master Lohan said.

I noticed Master Lohan drank only eggnog as we drove, and regularly went to a cooler in the trunk to get another quart of it when he ran out.

"Where do you get eggnog in June?" I asked.

"I have connections," he said.

"But isn't that kind of a holiday thing to drink?"

"It's Christmas in the southern hemisphere," he said.

I thought for a moment and said, "No, it's winter down there, but it's not Christmas."

"Good," he said. "Just wanted to see if you are thinking." He took another sip of the eggnog and kept driving south. We stopped at the beautiful Arches National Park in Utah, and looked at the amazing and gravity-defying stone arches. We camped out there for a few days. Master Lohan said nothing, but just went around with me looking at the rocks and arches and buttes. He also spent a lot of time meditating while I hiked on my own.

We then drove down to the Arizona border and spent the day at Monument Valley. I thought of all the old Westerns I had seen that were shot there. It was amazing to be here in person.

"You know how far away that butte is?" he said, pointing

to one of them.

"No," I said.

"I'll show you." He then took a large, red remote-control airplane out of the trunk, put it on the ground, and after some preparations, made it take off. He flew it over to the butte, the one that looked like a big mitten, and circled the plane around it. Then he made it fly to each of the remaining buttes, making one big circle over the valley.

"Do you know how to fly?" he asked.

"No," I said.

"Come here," he said, giving me the controls. "Just hold it like this, and it will circle again."

I held it, and we watched it circle around. It felt great to fly it, even though I wasn't doing much. He took the controls from me, made the plane land, and stowed it again. We got in the car, and headed off to New Mexico.

We got into New Mexico around nightfall, and stopped at a diner. We had not eaten all day and I was hungry. We sat down and were given menus, and then the waitress returned to take our order. Master Lohan had not looked at the menu at all.

"I'll have a hamburger," I said. The waitress turned to Master Lohan.

"What'll you have, honey?" she asked.

"Some food," Master Lohan said.

"Just … some food?" she said nervously. "Don't you want to order anything … in particular?"

"Anything is fine," he said.

"OK," she said, scratching her head with the pencil and looking confused. A few minutes later, she brought us each a hamburger. We ate quietly, and then got back on the road.

We drove another two hours, and still had not found a place to stay. We then went through a town where there was a variety of brand-name hotels on the main drag.

"Why not here? Or here?" I said, eager to get to sleep. "These places all look fine."

"They don't feel right," he said. "Too new."

We drove for what seemed like forever, and as I was about to fall asleep, we came across a run-down red-and-white motel in the middle of nowhere called the Sugata Inn. Its red-neon sign flashed "CANCY." We got out, stretched ourselves, and walked into the lobby. A heavy-set woman with dark hair and a pug nose was behind the glass doing a crossword puzzle. Standing next to her was an overweight man-child of about thirty, sucking on a popsicle stick, who stared at Master Lohan and me through his thick glasses as though we were two aliens from another planet who had just parked our spaceship outside.

"Need a room?" the woman asked.

"Yes," Master Lohan said.

"You're in luck. Rooms is all we got."

She filled out some forms, and slid paperwork to Master Lohan to sign.

"Where are our keys?" I asked.

"No keys," she said.

She came out from behind the glass and led us to our room, followed by the man-child sucking on frayed popsicle sticks.

"We got no locks on the doors here, which is why the rates is so low. You don't need locks out here, 'cause there ain't nobody 'round here anyway so you got nothin' to worry about. Nobody'll come in your room anyway, except maybe Edwin here. You might see him standin' over your bed in the middle of the night, but he don't mean no harm. He just not used to seein' people, that's all."

I gave Master Lohan a look. He patted me on the back.

"It'll be OK," he said. "This will do."

In the middle of the night I woke up, as a cold breeze swept through the room. I looked up and saw the door wide open. Edwin was standing at the head of my bed, eating an orange popsicle and staring at me and Master Lohan as if we were the most amazing thing he'd ever seen.

"Don't you have someplace to go?" I whispered pointedly at him, trying not to wake Master Lohan. He leaned over and looked at me and kept staring harder as if that could make him see better. I repeated my question, and he ran out of the room whining, still eating his popsicle. I closed the door, and pulled the covers over my head and went back to sleep.

We got up early the next morning, looked around, and nothing was missing. I guess Edwin just likes staring and doesn't take stuff. I asked Master Lohan if he saw him there.

"Yes," he said, "but you shouldn't have been so hard on him. I think you hurt his feelings."

We ate breakfast at a diner fifty miles up the road, and spent the day driving up to Colorado. At the end of the day, we found ourselves in the foothills of the Rockies. This was the one part of the trip I had prepared for. I had planned out a hike to the top of a small mountain, and had a compass and a map of where we were going. Master Lohan got out of the car, looked around, and took my compass gently away from me. He looked at the front and the back of it, and then threw it on the ground and crushed it under his foot.

"Hey! I spent twenty dollars on that!" I said.

"You never want to own something that can only point one way," he said. "You might get lost."

He began walking in his own direction, off the trail. I began to follow him. People were complaining and yelling that we were going off the path and weren't supposed to be hiking where we were. Before we knew it, we were going through people's backyards. We went through a few of them, and then I saw two Doberman pinschers barking in the yard in front of us, gnashing their teeth. Master Lohan walked calmly into the yard and sat down. The dogs came up and quietly began licking his hands. He began playing with them. He waved at me to come over, but I didn't. I was still thinking about my crushed compass and the hike I had planned. "The mountain is that way," I said to him, pointing behind me. He just smiled and kept playing with the dogs. "Best place to see mountain is from right here," he said.

By June 20, Master Lohan and I had ended up in Alliance, Nebraska, just in time for the summer solstice celebration at Carhenge, a replica of Stonehenge made out of wrecked cars painted silver and stuck into the ground in a circle. The next morning, along with about twenty other Carhenge devotees, we watched the sunrise amid the wrecked cars. Master Lohan had gotten up well before dawn and meditated throughout the sunrise. Others chanted and sang sacred songs. It was one of the most moving experiences of the trip.

We then headed north to Montana, and arrived in time to see the reenactment of Custer's defeat at the Battle of Little Bighorn. Master Lohan cheered for Crazy Horse and the Native Americans the whole time. He said he never missed it.

We then headed back south and then east and drove through Colorado and Kansas on I-70 and spent the night at a motel near the Colorado-Kansas border. We spent the next day driving through Kansas. Around noon, we turned off midway through the state, and Master Lohan drove to a store in the middle of nowhere—the biggest garden store I've ever seen. As soon as I walked in, I felt I had entered the center of the lawn maintenance universe. There was an incredible selection of double-curved spring-tined rakes, shovels, hoes, soil-moving machines, composters, hydroseeders, skid-mounted turf sprayers, dust controllers, multi-use atomizers, and new super-quiet leaf shredders and collectors that they let you try out right there.

"Master Lohan," I said, "I have a feeling I'm not in New Jersey anymore."

"You're not," he said, as he patted me on the back. Master Lohan had to drag me out of there by the hand.

We got off the highway when we entered Missouri, and were soon driving through the wine country along the Missouri River, when we crossed over the river and entered a town called Hermann. We pulled up to an ice cream shop in the center of town, which had a long line of families and kids waiting to get in. Master Lohan came out with a triple-scoop strawberry cone. I asked him why we had made the detour here. "Best strawberry ice cream in America. Go try." I went in and got some. He was right.

We got back on the road, and, driving along the Missouri River, I felt like calling my answering machine at home to see if there were any messages. I asked Master Lohan if he had a cell phone.

"Sure," he said, "here."

I started dialing. There was no service.

"Master Lohan, you don't have any service on this phone."

"I know."

"But why have a cell phone without any service?"

"Who would call?"

"So, why have one?"

"You have to have one these days, right? It's weird not to have a cell phone, isn't it?"

"Yes, but—"

I decided not to try to explain it to him.

We drove for over an hour, and then stopped at a field outside St. Louis where a group of people were flying remote-control airplanes. Master Lohan took his plane out, and flew it along with everyone else. Watching him again, I realized he was truly an expert—he could make it do loops, Immelmanns, perfect turns around trees that lined the field, and effortless landings. Some of the men stopped flying their planes just to watch him fly.

We then drove on to the Land Between the Lakes in Kentucky. We spent a few hours at the elk and bison prairie. Master Lohan got out of the car and walked up to the bison, who just stared quietly at him. He was breaking the rules. You weren't supposed to leave your car. I yelled at him to get back in, but he didn't listen to me. We stayed at the campground that night, and took off early the next morning.

As we drove through Kentucky in the early morning light, I couldn't stop looking at the rolling hills and bluegrass. It was so green and perfect. Who took care of all this? Did it just occur this way naturally? Or did horses graze on it to keep it so smooth? I realized I could never make a living here. But it was so beautiful. It made me think of the fall days back east and how green the grass became in the September rains, and the huge piles of leaves that we'd make by the end of the day.

"Master Lohan?" I asked.

"Yes, Kincaid?"

"Sometimes when I've raked all day, and there is a big pile of leaves, I check to see if anyone is looking, and if not, I jump in the pile and lie face up looking at the sky. I'm so tired from raking all day, but I look up and see the blue sky, and the white clouds, and the bare branches, and feel the wetness of the leaves against my coat and inhale their smell, which is like warm apple cider. When I'm exhausted like that, lying in the leaves, it doesn't matter that Kelly has left. It doesn't matter that I can't pay Mr. Leland the back rent because I spent it all on self-help seminars and that he may kick me out any day now. It doesn't matter that the people who own this house will call tomorrow and yell at me for the leaves I missed. Nothing matters. I don't need or want anything. I'm just happy to be looking at the sky and the waving branches and smelling the leaves. So, whenever I get happy like that, and I don't care about anything, I wonder, is there something wrong with me?"

"There's nothing wrong with anyone," he said.

We then drove all night as we headed up to Sandusky, Ohio, and the Cedar Point roller coasters. I had a nightmare that they had remade *Ben-Hur* starring Kevin Costner. I had visions of him smiling affably right before one of the races, flirting with a group of attractive Roman women. I awoke to see the green lawns and stately homes of Ohio, and in that bleary-eyed, half-awake state one can be in after a bad dream, asked Master Lohan,

"They didn't … remake *Ben-Hur* with Kevin Costner, did they?"

"No," he said, "they didn't. Rest easy."

We drove on to Cedar Point.

As Master Lohan and I rode on some of the biggest and fastest roller-coasters in the world, I wondered: are roller-coasters a symbol of how fast life goes by? Do they show the danger we must embrace if we are truly going to find ourselves? Master Lohan didn't say anything, but just sat in the front and yelled louder than any of the kids. What was he trying to tell me? I just looked over at him, and he smiled, and then started yelling again as the next ride began to go ninety miles an hour.

We then headed to Gettysburg, Pennsylvania. There was a convention of Lincoln impersonators that had taken over the Best Western where we were staying. As soon as we got to the hotel, an older, friendly-looking man named Ben came up to us.

"Where you two from?" he asked.

"New Jersey and Nevada," I said.

"Well, we don't have many Lincolns out in Nevada. Nice to have you here."

I tried at length to convince him that we weren't part of the convention, but he wouldn't have any of it.

"Our dinner starts in about an hour. You'll come in full costume, right?"

"No, we don't have costumes," I said. I thought that would

convince him we were not really part of the group.

"Oh, I always travel with extras. Come up to my room and I'll fit you both."

And before we knew it, we were in his room, and he was fitting us with Lincoln outfits to wear. Master Lohan looked great in his. The minute he put on his hat, he was transformed. We attended the dinner with all the other Lincolns, and found them all polite and friendly. They were of all ages, and came from all over the country. They spoke mostly about the past year, and where they had found the most work as Lincoln impersonators and educators. We were given a lot of advice on where to find impersonating work in Nevada and New Jersey.

"See you tomorrow for breakfast and the morning ceremony," Ben said to us at the end of dinner, as he headed upstairs to his room. "We all leave here at seven. Don't be late."

The next morning, we joined the rest of the group for breakfast, and then we walked up to the battlefield, all fifty or so of us. Lincolns of all sizes and shapes were there. White Lincolns, African-American Lincolns, Hispanic Lincolns, and a man no more than four feet tall, whose hat was half his height. Master Lohan and I walked in the back, looking at the different heights of the men and their hats bobbing up and down in the morning fog.

We all got to the field and stood there solemnly. Someone was supposed to recite the Gettysburg Address around this time. Apparently, no one had it memorized this year, nor did anyone remember to bring a copy. We all stood on the field quietly for ten minutes. Everyone looked around nervously.

Then, Master Lohan began speaking, and all the eyes of all the Lincolns turned to him:

> Four score and seven years ago our fathers brought forth on this continent, a new nation, conceived in Liberty, and dedicated to the proposition that all men are created equal.
>
> Now we are engaged in a great civil war, testing whether that nation, or any nation so conceived and so dedicated, can long endure. We are met on a great battle-field of that war. We have come to dedicate a portion of that field, as a final resting place for those who here gave their lives that that nation might live. It is altogether fitting and proper that we should do this.
>
> But, in a larger sense, we can not dedicate—we can not consecrate—we can not hallow—this ground. The brave men, living and dead, who struggled here, have consecrated it, far above our poor power to add or detract. The world will little note, nor long remember what we say here, but it can never forget what they did here. It is for us the living, rather, to be dedicated here to the unfinished work which they who fought here have thus far so nobly advanced. It

is rather for us to be here dedicated to the great task remaining before us—that from these honored dead we take increased devotion to that cause for which they gave the last full measure of devotion—that we here highly resolve that these dead shall not have died in vain—that this nation, under God, shall have a new birth of freedom—and that government of the people, by the people, for the people, shall not perish from the earth.

"He's a real Lincoln," Ben said, leaning over to me. "Knew it the minute I saw him. You too, I bet. And so's he," Ben said, nodding toward the four-foot-tall Lincoln. "You'd never know by looking at him. You should hear him do the Second Inaugural Address. The real thing, I tell you."

We left the field in silence and walked back to the hotel, getting stares from the busloads of tourists coming in for the day. Some kids threw candy at the four-foot-tall Lincoln, but he didn't even flinch.

Master Lohan and I left soon after, and drove on to New York. We went to a diner on Ninth Avenue called We're Out of That. After asking for three things they had run out of, Master Lohan ordered a cheeseburger and a vanilla shake. We talked a lot about the trip, and finally I asked him again how I could get Kelly back.

"Meditate," he said, eating his fries.

"That's it?" I asked.

"Yes," he said, "that's all you have to do."

I then asked him about the most important idea I had gotten out of his books, his Avoiding Yourself-Confronting Yourself Ratio, which he wrote about at length in *I'm OK, You're Not OK*. He said this ratio was the key to happiness—that by raising the amount of time you confronted yourself, you could increase your chances of knowing yourself and becoming happy on the deepest level.

"So, what percentage of the time do you think I confront myself?" I asked.

"Oh, maybe one percent of the time," he said. "But I get the sense that is better than where you have been."

"Where was I before?"

"Less than one percent," he said.

The next morning he woke me up early, and threw a basketball at me in bed.

"Time to get some exercise before the long flight to Spain," he said, and stood looking at me in a t-shirt, baggy shorts, and sneakers. We walked over to the West 4th Street Courts, and limbered up and waited with everyone else to be picked for a team.

"We got Lohan," a tall, muscular guy said, choosing him first as the picking started. I was chosen last, and ended up on the other team.

The game was physical, with lots of elbows flying, and I got bruised pretty badly, but Master Lohan was able to make lay-ups without anyone getting in his way. He seemed to have a magical ability to evade all the blocking with little effort. He also made nice three-point shots from the perimeter. I didn't play too well. I didn't know if I was just rusty or distracted by watching him play.

We then walked up 6th Avenue and looked into a yoga studio on 19th Street that was just ending its class. We stood there, and watched quietly as everyone sat cross-legged and chanted "Om" three times slowly.

"Do you know what 'Om' means?" Master Lohan asked me.

"No," I said, getting ready to receive a great teaching. This could be the most important moment of the trip, I thought.

"Neither do I," he said, and we started walking over to 5th Avenue.

Our last stop before the airport was a wedding Master Lohan was invited to, where the groom was one of his former students, he said.

We entered the church on 5th Avenue, Master Lohan showed his invitation, and we were led to our seats in the back. The usher gave us a rude stare for showing up in blue-and-black basketball garb while everyone else was dressed elegantly in pastel colors. There were about a hundred people in attendance, all in formal attire, and the inside of the church was beautifully decorated with flowers. The ceremony began, and the handsome young groom stood waiting at the altar in a gray Prince Edward morning coat. The bride, in an extravagant white gown, was escorted down the aisle by her father. The minister began the ceremony. He then arrived at the line,

"If there be anyone here today who objects to this union, let him now speak, or forever hold his peace."

"I object," Master Lohan said, standing up. The bride was aghast, and the groom turned toward Master Lohan with a perplexed expression on his face. The ceremony came to a halt. All eyes turned on us. Master Lohan passed the basketball clear across the church at the groom. He caught it. He looked down at the ball in his hand and smiled. Murmuring began to break out in the crowd. We left.

On our way to the airport, Master Lohan stopped at a newsstand in Manhattan and bought four lottery tickets. He then threw them right into the trash as we got in our cab.

"Why didn't you scratch them off first?" I asked.

"What's the point? I never win."

As we waited at the light, I saw a homeless man pull the lottery tickets out of the trash and start scratching them off. He seemed happy with the results, and put them in his pocket and ran off.

We then flew on to Pamplona, Spain for the festival of San Fermín and the Running of the Bulls. A few hours into the flight, we hit a lot of turbulence. Everyone was holding onto their seats with scared expressions, and a number of people got sick. I looked at Master Lohan next to me. He was sitting calmly with his eyes closed, as relaxed as I'd ever seen him. I closed my eyes and tried to relax like him. I couldn't. Finally, I said something, hoping he would say something to me and his calmness would transfer over.

THE POWER OF TWO WEEKS FROM NOW

"Pretty bumpy ride, huh?" I said.

"Yes," he said.

"Where does turbulence come from?" I asked.

"We are the turbulence," he said, without opening his eyes.

When Master Lohan said we would be running with the bulls, I knew I was becoming his true disciple. The turbulence at last ended, and as I watched the Atlantic below us, I was now looking forward to the day of the running, and seeing him charm the bulls out of his way. I imagined him walking serenely down the streets with the bulls, calming them as he had the Doberman pinschers and the bison.

When we arrived the next day, Master Lohan said I would be running by myself, while he would be standing in a terrace above watching the whole event. He said it was better this way, but didn't tell me why.

We spent the day before the run walking around the poor neighborhoods of Pamplona. I began to realize how I, even as a lawn worker, had more material possessions than any of these people. I told Master Lohan this, and said I did not feel I deserved all I had. He said he would be glad to take anything off my hands I didn't want, especially if I had a large-screen TV so he could watch the Phoenix Suns on something bigger than his thirteen-inch set.

On the morning of the run, I stood with hundreds of people waiting for the bulls to be released from the pen at the bottom of Santo Domingo Street. I heard everyone say, as is the custom, "We ask San Fermín, as our patron, to guide us through the *encierro* and give us his blessing." Then, the rocket went off, and the bulls were released. As I and everyone else ran frantically away from them, I thought of what a great lesson I was learning. The bulls probably represented my ego, or maybe the thoughts in my consciousness I needed to let go of in order to be free. Otherwise, I would live life gored by the horns of my own misconceptions. As I dodged the bulls who ran past me, or distracted them with the newspaper in my hand, I realized there is so much in life I have to avoid in order to end up in the ring of freedom one day. I then thought about Kelly. Maybe it didn't matter if she became a Rastafarian. I mean, I love her, not her hair. I was willing to put up with any kind of hair she wanted. It would just be a phase, anyway. It was okay if that was what she wanted. But then she never said she wanted it—I just thought she might because Cleo had become one. You know how women are. They do everything their friends do. I almost got gored by a large tan bull and then realized I had to stay totally in the present. I couldn't think about Kelly. I knew the main thing now was surviving the bull run, and just getting into the ring of freedom.

I glanced back and looked at all the bulls briefly. They now somehow all had blonde Rastafarian dreadlocks hanging off their heads. The locks were shaking in the breeze as the bulls ran toward me. I rubbed my eyes and looked back again, and the dreadlocks were gone. I decided not to look back anymore, and just ran straight for the ring.

As I arrived with the other survivors in the bullring, I realized that while bullfighting was a violent sport, violence was necessary to liberate your consciousness of illusions. It was a ruthless road to take to truly confront everything in me that was wrong, but it was necessary. Master Lohan was right to bring me there. I realized that the bulls were my friends. They were actually helping me to see what in my consciousness needed to go, and where I needed to yield in order to see the truth. I had arrived in the ring unscathed, except for a few cuts and bruises from where I had fallen down on the run along the old streets. I heard the cheering crowd, and realized that this was the reward of being on the path to enlightenment and being willing to face your monsters head-on. Right then I decided to call Kelly when I got home, except I had no idea where she was or how to contact her.

On the plane ride home, I asked Master Lohan what the running with the bulls meant. Was it about running from my ego? What did the bulls represent? Were they an ancient Buddhist god embodied by wild animals meant to ruthlessly cut away my dangerous illusions? He said he had brought me here just because he liked to see how much interesting stuff he could get me to do. I knew this was just his way of hiding the real meaning of the bull run from me, and that it was too early in our work for me to understand. I tried to figure it out, but I couldn't.

Having just put my life in danger, and thinking about

mortality, I asked Master Lohan, "What would you do if you had only two weeks to live?"

He thought for a moment, and said, "I would sit in my hospital bed and fly a remote-control plane that I would have a friend release at a major league ballpark during a game. I would love to watch the umpires chase it around as I made it land and take off from my hospital bed. With any luck, I could knock an umpire's hat off."

"That's all?" I asked.

"Yes," he said. "What else would I do?"

Two Weeks

Relieving Depression in America

Remember to enjoy yourself while you are depressed.
—Master Lohan

When I arrived home after the trip, I felt a bit let down. It was an amazing experience, and I was sad that it was over. But I realized this is a normal response, and that I was just one of the many people feeling blue in America at that moment.

Depression is a major problem in America. Each year in our country, depression is partly or entirely responsible for:

- 921,973 unneeded shopping sprees, resulting in 752,251 unnecessary purchases, including 532,404 pairs of shoes, 251,234 pairs of pants, and 62,430 sweaters.
- The consumption of 14,572,402 donuts, cupcakes, and other snack foods, eaten impulsively for non-hunger-related reasons.

- 223,721 primetime TV shows missed due to depression-related arguments.
- 156,256 uncleaned messes accumulating because it "just doesn't matter."

With statistics like these, a solution must be found. Thankfully, denial can help.

While many mental health professionals suggest confronting depression head-on in order to solve it, denying it is an even better idea. The most effective way I have found to help people deny their depression is to encourage them to somehow alter their outward appearance. This can include makeup, a new hairstyle, or, if they can be afforded, calf implants.

CALF ENHANCEMENT

While facelifts were once all the rage, calf implants are now ascending in popularity in Los Angeles as a way to make people feel better. The good news is that they can be had for as little as three thousand dollars per calf. Calf implants can play a valuable role in lifting our mood and getting to the cause of depression, which often stems from having smaller calves than others. Start by getting only one calf implant, and tell your friends at the gym as you walk around in shorts that maybe it's about time you started working on that other leg.

RELIEVING DEPRESSION BY BECOMING JEWISH

Another way to fight depression is by becoming Jewish. To become a Jew, in this sense, does not mean you need to take on any new beliefs or adopt any Jewish cultural traditions. You merely need to act and think like other Jews and use their methods of social interaction.

Jews are rarely depressed. They may be worried, guilty, envious, greedy, joyous, spiteful, carefree, narcissistic, or megalomaniacal—but never depressed. This is because the very nature of being a Jew doesn't allow it. The only Jews who become depressed are those who have abandoned their Judaism and are imitating Protestants.

If you find yourself depressed, ask yourself these questions:
- Have you returned anything to a store recently and complained?
- How much bargaining do you do on a daily basis?
- Have you argued with a perfect stranger about something trivial in the past two weeks?
- Have you told a detailed story in mixed company about any suffering you have experienced recently? Jews have a natural ability to feel that their suffering is of interest to everyone. Thus, by talking about it, they share it, feel relieved, and become happier as a result. Non-Jews need to follow their example.

If you have not been doing any of the above, you may be suffering from a deficiency of being Jewish, which in turn can lead to depression.

How is this? What is the nature of being a Jew?
To be a Jew means to annoy other people with an open heart. This is why Jews don't meditate—they prefer to go bother other people instead, but they do it with love. They love to annoy you. This is how they engage you and begin a relationship from their heart.

Jews are not always outgoing people. Often, they are quite shy by nature. It is only through their skills in annoying others that they are able to make friends. Often, marriages of Jews are based on the mutual ability of a couple to annoy each other into feeling alive. It is why these marriages last so long.

Also, when Jews go out to meet others, they don't merely talk about one thing. To a Jew, all things in their life are connected. For example, when bargaining, they don't simply ask for a lower price—they tell their life story, how their husband is out of work, how the son is a nogoodnik, and how the daughter married a bum, so they can't afford the price you are asking. So, how low can you make it now? they ask. They don't just want a bargain. They want a friend who knows everything about them.

How can I use being Jewish to fight my depression?
Realize that, first and foremost, Jews do not sit in their homes

contemplating the meaning of life or their role in the universe. Jews go out and put themselves in the middle of as much commotion as possible. They deny they are depressed and just walk out the door. This is why they are so happy.

If you're a gentile, and life has begun to lose its zest, you may just sit at home, shrinking into your own world and getting blue, watching soap operas and taking antidepressants. But if you were a Jew, you'd do this instead: you'd think of something you bought recently, a dress or a suit that didn't fit right, and reevaluate it closely. You'd pull it out of the closet and look at it and realize the hem doesn't look right. You would then take it back to the store and complain to the clerk for an hour or so. This can make for a very full and enjoyable day, as you can then go to your friends' houses and tell them all the struggles you had with a troublesome shopkeeper.

In order to be a Jew, make sure to buy things from people who actually make them themselves—in small shops, if possible. When you complain, the idea is to develop a relationship, not just vent to someone with no authority. The fact that over forty percent of retail dollars in America are now spent in large chain stores is the reason so many people are depressed—we can't complain and start relationships as we used to in the past. The domination of such large corporate entities in the retail world is another way that Jews and their cultural traditions and social customs are being pushed off the American landscape.

I want to complain, but am surrounded by nature. What is there to complain about?
Plenty. Trees, for example. They take up all that space, don't pay taxes, and are generally antisocial.

I want to become Jewish and feel happier right away. How do I start?
Bargaining or complaining is the way. The next time you buy something, don't be a nebbish and pay the regular price, haggle—even at Sears. Perhaps one of the managers can bargain with you. Find a flaw in one of their appliances. Perhaps some of the large chain stores could have survived the latest economic upheaval if the salespeople were allowed to haggle.

THE BUDDHA MEETS THE RABBI

Imagine what would happen if the Buddha met a Rabbi and tried to explain nothingness to him.

"You want nothingness? Look at my grandson," the Rabbi answered.

"He is enlightened?" asked the Buddha excitedly.

"No. He didn't even go to graduate school. He has a lousy job that barely pays the rent. Look at him!"

"Material goods are not needed. Emptiness arrives only after years of meditation, though sometimes the realization happens sooner," the Buddha says. "Then, the whole of reality opens up to you. Emptiness."

"That's it—nothing? I should get excited about nothing?"

"No," the Buddha said, "nothingness allows everything to come to you for a fuller experience."

"Everyone is coming over? I like this."

"No," the Buddha said, "Emptiness. Lack of ego."

"Lack of ego. And if I am not for myself, who will be for me?" the Rabbi said, looking sadly into the distance.

Two Weeks

Denial Cookies

The secret of life is honesty and fair dealing. If you can fake that, you've got it made. –GROUCHO MARX

Denial can really make you work up an appetite. It takes extra effort to suppress things, and then remember what you've suppressed. But while doing all this denial, you don't want to admit to having eaten anything, especially sugary, high-fat snacks. What's left to eat? Nothing is better than a batch of Denial Cookies. They're easy to make:

Denial Cookies

Ingredients:
5 cups all-purpose flour
2 teaspoons baking soda
2 teaspoons salt
2 cups butter, softened

1½ cups granulated sugar
1½ cups firmly packed brown sugar
4 eggs
2 teaspoons vanilla extract
2 packages semi-sweet chocolate morsels (24 oz.)
2 cups nuts, chopped

Directions:
Preheat oven to 375° F.

In a large bowl, combine flour, baking soda, and salt; set aside.

In a large mixing bowl, beat softened butter, granulated sugar, and brown sugar together until creamy. Taste often to make sure it has the right sweet-and-smooth consistency.

Add eggs, one at a time, tasting after each addition. Blend in vanilla extract. Taste again.

Gradually beat in flour mixture. Taste often to make sure it has the right cakey, sweet mouthfeel.

Stir in semi-sweet chocolate morsels and chopped nuts. Now take it out into the living room and consume as much as needed to make sure it has the right taste while watching your favorite TV shows or movie. You may also leave cookie dough in the refrigerator for up to two weeks and snack on it before baking. Taste often to make sure it hasn't gone bad.

Bake remainder by dropping rounded measuring tablespoonfuls onto cookie sheets; cool completely.

Yields: *About 3 cookies.*

You Are Not Your Possessions

---∽∾∽---

Always choose the path of greatest resistance.
—Master Lohan

I was recently sitting with a group of friends watching something they called "a football game" on a large-screen television. Everyone seemed to be enjoying "the game" as it built towards its exciting climax. The score was "tied" and everything seemed to hinge on the upcoming "plays," as they were called by those present. It was just then that I realized that what we were watching was not really a game, but a series of light pixels dancing on a TV screen. We believed in the illusion of the game, but it was not really there. To the great dismay of everyone present, I then went up and unplugged the set and the satellite feed. Our trip back to reality can be hard, I realized, and not everyone can make it smoothly, but we had to start at some point. I was then ushered from the house brusquely, and told never to return, while the men frantically tried to reconnect the TV to watch what they considered their "reality." As I picked myself up off the pavement and looked at my broken glasses, I knew that someone had been helped today by being forced to come closer to the world we all live in, even if the suddenness of it was unpleasant for them.

Two Weeks

The insight I just shared is something we are all capable of. We can become much more connected to reality if we desire it deeply enough. We are often not aware of the power of our perceptive abilities. For example, if you arrive home late at night and see your elderly uncle on the couch asleep with the TV on, and you turn it off, and he wakes up and says, "Hey, I was watching that," it is because his sense of what was going on in his environment was much more keenly attuned than you realize. Like a mountain lion quietly moving through the forest, your uncle was deeply connected to everything around him even while asleep, and the slightest change in his environment was something he could notice. We all possess these abilities, and only need to cultivate our senses as our elders have in order to arrive at this advanced level of connectedness to the world.

Two Weeks

Monks are well known for their keen connectedness to the world around them. This reminds me of a story of two monks who approach a river one day and see a woman waiting by the shore. "Will you carry me over?" she asks. "I cannot swim and without your help I will drown trying to cross." The first monk says no, as he took a vow never to touch a woman. The second monk shrugs and says he would be happy to, and carries her across. He then places her down on the other side, and the two monks continue on their way. Soon after, the first monk asks, "Why did you break your vows and touch that woman?" The second monk says, "I didn't break any vows. I made sure not to take that vow so I can touch women." The message is clear: Read the fine print before joining any religious organization, and only join those that allow you a line-item veto on any rules.

Two Weeks

How to Use Denial in Our Everyday Lives

Who are you going to believe, me or your own eyes?
—Groucho Marx

THE MEDITATION OF DENIAL

The most important way to use denial on a daily basis is to make sure that we are meditating with the correct word. Master Lohan taught me that all those who live in denial no longer meditate on the word "Om," but instead say, as they sit in the cross-legged lotus position with their palms facing upward toward heaven:

Nooooooooooooooooooooooooooooo

This includes Wall Street swindlers, corrupt corporate officers, and those in government who are not telling us the truth. They usually meet in a large, designated meditation room, dim the lights, and say this word together until they are all united in denial. Meditating on this word day and night helps keep them in their altered state of mind. See if it doesn't work for you.

I am now developing an audio series designed to help you forget and deny almost anything you like. Using a series of mnemonic devices, these CDs will help you retain nothing from important meetings, parties, and other life events, leaving your mind completely blank at all times and free to think anything you like. This unique program will allow you to ignore almost anything you desire with ease.

OTHER WAYS TO USE DENIAL

- Pretend not to know what a word means. Remember when President Clinton during testimony said, in answer to a question, "That depends on what the meaning of the word 'is' is"? You can use this technique as well. When your personal trainer says to do 40 crunches a day, tell her at your next session that you thought that she meant eat 40 crunchy foods per day, and that you picked corn chips. Give an innocent shrug when she weighs you and says you gained four pounds this week. Blame her for not expressing herself with greater clarity.
- Another time to use denial is when you are the head of

some great corporation that is beginning to sink. You know things look dire, but in the back of your mind you know that you will still get a large bonus when you leave no matter what you do. So, spend like there is no tomorrow. This will create the illusion of success at your company. Take all your executive friends on lavish vacations. This delusional behavior can greatly inspire the rank-and-file employees into believing all is well.
- Play the game "Pentagon" at your next party. Pentagon is easy to play. You need three or more players, and before the start of the game, one person is chosen to be the Pentagon. The game begins. Everyone gives all the money they have to the person playing the Pentagon. Then everyone says, "Where is our money?" The person playing the Pentagon shrugs and says, "I don't know." Then the game is over. The person playing the Pentagon gets to keep all the money. In this game, it is most advantageous to be the person playing the Pentagon.

CONSIDER JOINING A CULT

If you are truly committed to denying all aspects of reality, the best thing to do is join a cult. There are many cults in America, and they are friendlier and easier to join than ever. Simply check the Yellow Pages under "Cults," and pick the one that seems right for you.

Here are some of the benefits of joining a cult:
- You will finally be surrounded by people who will keep you from ever having to see reality clearly on your own.
- All your thinking is done for you. You no longer need to engage in any "dialectical" conversations where you have to think critically about your position or your opponent's. There will be easy answers to all your questions about life and death, and if you don't understand, that's okay! You're not supposed to.
- You won't be plagued with money worries, as cults like to take it all from you.
- No more spending time alone—which is dangerous! You could start thinking for yourself and who knows where that could lead. Cults supply you with a cadre of ready-made zombielike friends who will all think the same thoughts along with you, few of which will have any significant connection with reality.
- Life will be exciting, because in a cult, the end of the world is always near. No more having to work out your salvation or enlightenment over a lifetime—it's always crisis time! This makes your former life, which was overrun with mundane tasks like walking the dog and paying bills, seem boring.

Best of all, cults are safer than ever these days since they discovered that mass suicides are bad for membership. They also create bad press and reduce the income for the organization. Ultimately, it is money and power that the people at the top want, not to harm you, their follower. So not to worry!

∽∾

STARTING A CULT

For the intrepid folks out there bored with the current selection of cults in America, consider starting your own. You'll need only a few followers at first, but before you know it, your house will be surrounded by an FBI SWAT Team. All you need is a series of strange beliefs and the ability to help others believe in them. Pick up a copy of Hildegard Benson's classic, *Starting a Cult for Fun and Profit!*

∽∾

JOIN AMERICA'S ECONOMIC DENIAL

Ever since America took the dollar off the gold standard, we have printed our money without backing it with a precious metal to guarantee its value. Since then, the value of our money is something imaginary that we all agree upon. Since taking America off the gold standard, our budget deficit has gone up markedly. In other words, our government spends a lot more money than it takes in, the value of which is a collective dream. Is this a problem?

Of course not.

Two Weeks

Is Suffering Meaningful?

Maybe.

If we look deeply enough, we find that the answer depends on the kind of suffering we are experiencing. Some suffering can be very meaningful and teach us a great deal about ourselves and our lives. It can deepen our awareness about the human experience and teach us compassion and understanding. In other instances, it can be a complete waste of time. Thus, suffering falls into two categories. Let us look at these two kinds of suffering in detail.

TWO KINDS OF SUFFERING

The first kind of suffering is called *Fruitful Suffering*. It is essential to our growth physically, emotionally, psychologically, and spiritually. Without this kind of suffering, it is unlikely that we would learn to understand what pain is, be able to empathize with others, or work to minimize hardship in the world at large. In this sense, our suffering is fruitful because it makes us more developed and deeper as individuals, and helps us make the world a better and more compassionate place.

Being a prisoner, enduring a job we don't like, going through a bad marriage, or even being raised by people who can't remember our first name are all forms of suffering that can lead us to a more profound experience of human existence. This is all *Fruitful Suffering*.

The second kind of suffering is called *Waste of Time Suffering*. This is when we are stopped by a policeman and given a ticket for not signaling for a turn, attend a boring party or meeting, or are asked to go shopping with our wives while they take forever trying on outfits that all look the same to us, and continually ask our opinion about each of them. We are also expected to remember outfits long after they have been taken off and compare them with ones now being worn. This suffering does not lead to any kind of growth or insight into ourselves or the world, and hence is called *Waste of Time Suffering*.

The problem with *Waste of Time Suffering* is that it keeps you from experiencing *Fruitful Suffering*. The goal in life is always to either be in a state of pleasure or in *Fruitful Suffering*, and to avoid the dreaded dead zone in the middle which is *Waste of Time Suffering*. The point is to make your suffering as

IS SUFFERING MEANINGFUL?

fruitful as possible, and when it is over, focus on having as good a time as you can. It is a life of extremes we seek, not the boring "middle way."

For example, no great books have ever been written about a man watching his wife decide which dress to buy. Yet many great books have been written by those who have been kept in prisoner of war camps for years. The point is to leave the shopping mall as soon as possible and enlist in the army so that you can experience *Fruitful Suffering*. You will then be pushed to the very brink of human existence and write that great novel which encompasses every exalted and noble literary theme there is. This novel will in turn earn enough royalties to cover the bills for all the clothes your significant other likes to buy.

Other Areas Where We Need to Stay the Course with Denial

From a certain point onward there is no longer any turning back. That is the point that must be reached.
—Franz Kafka

WHO NEEDS A MOUNTAIN?

Mountaintops are now being routinely destroyed to harvest coal. This leads to terrible environmental destruction. Yet, scientists tell us that we have thousands of mountains left, so there is no danger of them becoming extinct. And as long as we don't know about this mountaintop destruction and the horrendous effects it has on surrounding communities, we don't need to worry about it.

REPORTING IS OBSOLETE

There once was a time when reporters used to venture into the field and brave dangerous conditions to gather stories. This is no longer the case. Today, Pentagon officials and other government leaders escort the media about, and tell them what to print. Word is that the Pentagon is creating a room with large flat-screen TVs to show reporters what is going on in battlefields across the world, eliminating the need to ever endanger their lives again while reporting.

PESTICIDES ARE PERFECT

We are told the pesticides we use on our lawn have only benefits, and are free of side effects. Never mind that when used regularly, they may increase the chance of birth defects, according to published studies. I am forced to say along with my customers that the most important thing is that a lawn be free of weeds, and that we ignore whatever other effects these chemicals may have.

INFRASTRUCTURE? WHO NEEDS IT?

Many people say that America is in danger of losing its infrastructure, as its bridges and other structures weaken and disintegrate, and that this is a dire situation. This is actually a great opportunity for Detroit. It will allow American auto manufacturers to bring back their muscle cars. As the bridges fail and collapse, we'll need plenty of engine power to be able to accelerate to a high enough speed to jump over the rivers and ravines these bridges once spanned.

WHAT THIRD PARTY?

Americans need to stay unaware that there are any other political parties besides the two major, corporate-sponsored ones. If a third party were introduced, and its candidates allowed into major debates, it could lead to real discussions of actual issues. This amount of substance would confuse the average American as well as the mainstream candidates. And isn't there enough confusion already?

HURRICANES? WHERE?

There are people in Louisiana who claim a hurricane came through their state in August of 2005. There is no evidence that such a hurricane actually occurred.

What is more, we need to stop forecasting hurricanes altogether. By denying they exist from the beginning, we can eliminate many of the repairs and other costly measures that are often needed in their wake. By forecasting them, we are admitting that they exist, and are only asking for more trouble.

PRETENDING TO HOLD A CHICAGO MAYORAL ELECTION

Every four years, the people of Chicago pretend to participate in a competitive election for the job of mayor. Yet everyone knows that as long as he wants the job, Richard M. Daley will remain in office. Since no real candidate knows he or she has a chance against the enthroned Mayor Daley, past candidates that have gone up against him include a broken sextant, a box of used fan belts, and a twelve-year-old boy.

WHO NEEDS TOPSOIL?

Our topsoil in the breadbasket of the country is wearing thin, but our food still looks great, so there is no need to worry. Should the soil blow away, we could have another dustbowl, but that will just make us all nostalgic for the 1930s, so there is nothing to be concerned about.

OTHER AREAS WHERE WE NEED TO STAY THE COURSE WITH DENIAL

WHAT MISSING TRILLIONS?

On September 10, 2001, Secretary of Defense Donald Rumsfeld held a press conference and said that over two trillion dollars in Pentagon funds were missing. Rumsfeld said that "according to some estimates, we cannot track 2.3 trillion dollars in transactions." That's $8,000 for every man, woman, and child in this country. In a report by the Inspector General, the Pentagon admitted it cannot account for twenty-five percent of what it spends. Yet, as flag-clutching Americans, we should not get too upset when the Pentagon misplaces large sums. We should let them focus entirely on creating complex weapons systems and invading easy-to-beat countries, which are their strong points, and not ask them to count money, which, unless you have a calculator, is much more challenging. Imagine asking the Pentagon to be fiscally accountable in times like these, when our soldiers are defending freedom around the globe! Plus, what would the average American do with $8,000? Probably spend it on the mortgage, food, or higher education. Now, that's waste! These are trivial uses when compared to our government's need to lose large sums, which, when done correctly, is said to help keep morale at the Pentagon high.

UFOs: EVEN IF YOU SEE ONE, THEY DON'T EXIST

There are two instances in which we must deny the existence of UFOs. The first is if we've actually seen one. The second is if we haven't. In either case, we must continue to say they were never there in any way, shape, or form.

Why? We know from all alien movies (except *E.T.*) that they want to destroy us, so the rule with UFOs is to shoot first so there is no need to ask any questions later. Then call your local Air Force so they can come by, pick up all the evidence, and do a nice job of suppressing everything.

More reasons to deny the existence of interstellar illegal aliens:

- Awareness of peaceful worlds out there could lead to a peaceful period on earth, which is bad news for weapons manufacturers.
- We may derive new energy technologies from them that could greatly reduce our need for oil—not good if there are oil stocks in your retirement fund.

So, if an alien spaceship lands on your front lawn, give them the cold shoulder. Don't talk to them no matter how nice they may seem, or how long they traveled to get to your door. It only encourages them. This may seem rude at first, but we have to be unified about this. Make sure to pick up the government pamphlet, "How to Ignore a UFO."

WHOM SHOULD WE BLAME THE ECONOMIC CRISIS ON?

While some suggest the cause is aggressive hedge fund managers, subprime mortgages, or a lack of government oversight of Wall Street, the real person to blame for the economic crisis is the actor Alec Baldwin. His financial overconfidence, displayed in roles he has played in films such as *Glengarry Glen Ross,* has created hordes of ravenous consumers who in turn have brought about the rising bankruptcies and credit card debt that have brought our economy to its knees.

Look around your life right now. Whom can you blame your problems on? How does it make you feel to have those responsibilities taken from you? Liberated? Happy? Feeling lighter? Stay with that feeling. Denial and blaming others for the problems we have created can only bring joy.

Two Weeks

How To (Temporarily) Conquer Illness with Denial

Sometimes you have to look reality in the eye, and deny it. —Garrison Keillor

If you have a serious illness of any kind, denial can be your best friend.

The point of any life-threatening ailment is to use it to entertain those around you. Perhaps you have a tumor on your neck. Instead of getting radiation and chemotherapy, ignore the tumor and let it grow. Then, if your job involves having someone fill out paperwork in front of you, wait for them to say, "Isn't that a big tumor on your neck?" Then take out a pocket mirror and look at it and say, "Oh my God!" and run out of the room. Watch their reaction from a crack in the door. Later, you can recall these incidents and laugh about them with your friends.

If you have cancer, it is important not to undergo any kind of treatment such as chemotherapy. Chemotherapy causes hair loss, and such hair loss creates undue misery for others. Those that visit you will worry that they, too, may one day lose all their hair. No one likes to confront hair loss and find out what their bald scalp looks like. This is especially true for white men, who will never look as good bald as African-Americans. Cancer reveals, therefore, that white men are not as cool as they think. This is the last thing they want to face, and it is a cruel realization to force upon the fragile white male ego.

If you must receive chemotherapy, wear a wig. Ideally, have two, and when visiting relatives leave the room for a moment, change from brunette to blonde and see if they notice upon their return. If they don't, take them out of your will.

If you're in the hospital dying of some dreaded disease with only a few days to live, act as though this was all your idea in the first place. Start complaining about how bad things are today, and say who would want to live anyway what with the price of baseball tickets, not to mention the lack of good help in shoe stores and how much they charge for a decent sandwich in diners. Plus, there is hardly any meat in them. Make it seem like leaving this life is no big deal and the foolish ones are those who stay around.

Most of all, don't let disease affect your mood. Yes, you may be dying, but as terrible as death is, it's good to get it out of the way as soon as possible. This way it's not hanging over your head for years to come. Imagine having to go through countless years of a long, fulfilling, and enjoyable life only to have to face this in the end. Not you. You're doing it now, and you know the saying, "Do what you don't like first."

If that doesn't cheer you up, consider all the things you've gotten away with during your life that you were never caught doing. That ought to put a smile on your face. And, if you haven't yet done anything that you were afraid of being caught doing, now's the time.

HELPING THOSE IN NEED

Often, I visit the sick and infirm to help give them peace. I remember recently sitting with a young man, the son of a friend of mine, who plays high school basketball. He was bedridden in the local hospital with a badly twisted ankle and in need of comfort. After sitting in his presence meditating for an hour and transmitting my peace to him, something finally moved in him, and he desperately blurted out, "What are you doing here?"

It is often the person with the quiet presence such as myself who is not appreciated. The work that meditators do can seem meaningless or out of step with a world that values busyness and accomplishments. It often seems we meditators are doing nothing all day. We do nothing to stimulate the economy. We don't do tangible things like building houses. We seem meaningless.

As he kept yelling "What are you doing here?" I began to more deeply explore why all of us are here and what our true purpose is. As I did, the nurse ushered me out of the room and out through the front of the hospital. I looked at an ambulance pulling up. I kept meditating. An old woman was being taken out on a stretcher. The ambulance driver told me the woman was conscious, but had recently had a stroke. And what is a stroke, but blood and plaque blocking the arteries that feed the brain? I thought how uncanny the resemblance was between her and me. I do not fit in the hospital room. Her blood does not fit in her brain. We are all more similar and connected than we know.

As I stood there sending her peaceful thoughts, her gurney collided with my leg. She looked at me with anger and extended the middle finger of her right hand toward me. In some cultures, this can be interpreted as a highly abusive and critical gesture, but not to me. It sent me deep into a cascade of thought. I sought to fully understand what she meant by this. I opened my eyes and watched the gurney go into the hospital, her hand still outstretched towards me with the same gesture. And I finally understood what she was telling me: You are on the middle way. The right path. Stay there. Continue with what you are doing. You are helping people.

Two Weeks

Watching the Ballgame

There is only one crime, and that is to have the opportunity to love someone, and not love them.
—Master Lohan

After a long day of raking, I started thinking about Master Lohan. I hadn't spoken to him in a while. The last conversation we had was about Kelly. I replayed it in my head.

"Master Lohan, you said if I meditated a lot, it would bring Kelly back. It hasn't."

"I know. So how do you like meditating?"

"You lied to me?"

"Sure. Do you like meditation?"

"Yes, but—"

"So? Why complain? She is never coming back. Maybe this can be your new focus."

I thought about this for a while, and then went and meditated for twenty minutes, just sitting quietly. I did like it.

He was right. Maybe I should just deny that I knew anyone named Kelly in the first place.

I then got up and looked through the mail. There was a letter from her. I opened it and read it. She was coming home for a visit soon. Wow. I hadn't seen her in nine months. I began wondering how it would be to have her around again. What would she be like? Would she notice all the personal growth I had gone through? Would she like how I had redone the hedges in the front? What would we be like together? Was she coming back to stay with me, or with Cleo?

To get my mind off her, I started watching baseball on TV. Diamondbacks vs. Cardinals. There was an interruption in the game because some baloney-head was flying a remote-control plane around the outfield. The players were standing around looking annoyed. There was an indefinite delay of game while they tried to catch it. It was landing and taking off on the grass, and just as the umpires would get close enough to grab it, it would take off again.

Actually, it was kind of funny. Whoever was at the controls really knew what he or she was doing. And having fun, too. You knew every little kid watching the game was laughing. They showed close-ups of kids in the stands cracking up behind their gloves. Even some of the Cardinal players were breaking their stone-faced expressions and smiling. Especially when the plane swooped low and knocked off an umpire's hat, and made him stamp the ground. A few players from both sides jumped out of their dugouts and cheered when that happened.

Then, suddenly, after knocking off the umpire's hat, the plane petered out, and made a sudden, awkward landing in the outfield. A player walked up to it and held it up for everyone like a caught lobster. The crowd went wild.

Master Lohan. I didn't know where he was. I called all the hospitals in Las Vegas, and with some finagling, found where he was by saying I was a relative. I booked a flight out for that night.

The next day I arrived at his hospital. His bed was empty. There was a remote-control device for a model airplane on his nightstand that was plugged into a wireless card. I asked around, and found out that he had passed away the night before. I finally spoke to his doctor.

"What did he die of?"

"I don't know. He was the one who told us he was dying. He was perfectly healthy according to all our tests. But he said he didn't want to inconvenience anyone, or something like that, and that he should be here, so we admitted him. Here, there's something you may want to see."

He pointed to a cardboard box in the corner with the return address of Hermann, Missouri.

"Now, he ate a gallon of strawberry ice cream the last day of his life—do you think he was trying to cure himself?"

He turned and looked directly at me.

"You don't look Korean. Are you family?" he asked.

"No," I said.

"Well, have some ice cream anyway, there's a ton of it left. He got some for the whole floor."

The nurse handed me a dish of strawberry ice cream. She was eating some robotically herself. I looked at it, but felt too guilty to have some. They left me alone in the room. I looked at the remote control device, and wanted to laugh, and felt guilty about that. I collapsed into the chair.

Then I remembered his three rules. If you find something funny, I do not object to you laughing. If you are tired, I do not object to you resting. If you are hungry, I do not object to you eating.

I ate the ice cream and rested a while, looking out the window at the red mountains of Las Vegas. I smiled. He had done it. He had interrupted a major league baseball game. He had knocked off an umpire's hat. His life was complete.

It then started to hurt, in my chest. It hurt really bad. I leaned against the wall, and was surprised at how much pain I was in. I sat down. I missed him a lot. He was like a—I don't know, like a Master Lohan. He was unlike anyone I had ever met.

Why did he have to leave?

The pain in the center of my chest deepened. I realized this was what caring was—a lot of pain in the center of your chest area when someone leaves. It kept hurting more. And more.

I sat there for an hour, and then talked to the nurse again. I found out that he had left instructions to be cremated. I drove over to the crematorium. I walked in, and asked the man behind the counter, who was engrossed in reading a newspaper, whether he knew anything about a man named Lohan and any instructions he had left.

"Oh, that one, yes—he just wanted to be cremated and then thrown out in the trash. So that's what we did."

"You just—threw him out?" I asked.

"Sure. We do whatever you want here. We can even shoot you into space if you got the coin." He noticed how upset I was. "You a relative?"

"No. I mean, sort of—"

He gave me a quizzical look and started to go back to his paper.

"Look," I said, "I have to find out where those ashes are. You don't know where I could find them, do you?"

"They were taken away in the trash today, and are probably just lying in the city dump right now." He paused. "You know, that's the first time anybody's requested that—just to be burned up and thrown out. I thought he must be a criminal or something. Was he?"

"No," I said.

"Yeah, right," he said, and went back to his paper.

I drove back to the airport, and I couldn't believe no one knew where his ashes were. On the flight home, I looked out the window and thought about how we had driven across the land I was now flying over. I thought about how much fun we'd had. I saw Monument Valley not long after we took off. As we flew over Nebraska, I had a strong desire to go to

Carhenge. That is where his ashes should be. At least we should do a ceremony for him there. But who would come? And there wasn't time. Kelly would be home any day now.

Back in Town

He who hesitates is found.
—Master Lohan

Two days after getting home from Las Vegas, Kelly returned. I was glad I had those two days to pull myself back together. I didn't want her to see me all sad. I don't think she's ever seen me that way. Men have to be strong at all times or they are not men, as Wendell Vance would say.

Around noon, I heard a horn honking and went outside. There they were. They pulled up in Cleo's car. Cleo waved to me from the driver's seat. Kelly got out. I looked at her. She looked incredible. The most beautiful woman in the world—easily. Other women are a candle in the sun compared to her. She took off her sunglasses, folded them into her purse, and looked at me.

She had gone Rastafarian.

She walked up to me and smiled. "What do you think?" she said, twirling around so I could see the new her.

"It looks great," I said. "Blonde dreadlocks. They suit you." I could see she wanted a reaction out of me. I stayed calm and just smiled.

She looked at me, taking me in.

"You look great," she said. "Lots of color in your skin. Raking a lot?"

"Yeah," I said. "You look nice, too. Mexico has been good to you."

"So, what's new with you? Doing any personal growth, or just hanging around as usual?"

"Nothing much," I said, trying to be mysterious. Don't touch the lava. Eat some vegetables. Follow the rules. Learn how to use the copier. I was trying to remember everything at once. My mind went blank.

"Just like you," she said, "doing nothing."

"Yeah, nothing," I said. "Not that you can do anything anyway," I said.

"Yeah, you can't do anything," she said.

I kissed her. She smiled.

I looked at her again while I held her. She had evolved a lot in nine months. She had this glow in her eyes from all the strange places she had been. She had done amazing things, I could tell—lived in the wilderness, danced with snakes, studied with a shaman, smoked strange and dangerous weeds—who knows what. She was completely different. But somehow the same. And happy.

It was so frustrating. I try to catch up with her, and she runs a mile ahead of me. How could I ever meet up with her if she keeps evolving like this? Couldn't she just agree not to evolve for a while so I could catch up with her and we could finally be in the same place? You can't just keep endlessly evolving, especially when you have a head start. This keeps the one you love forever out of reach. It's not very courteous.

"I love you," I said.

"Yeah?" she said, smirking. She looked me up and down, walked around me. "How do you know? You don't know what love is."

"Oh, I know," I said.

"You do?" she said. "There's something different about you, that's for sure."

"What?" I said.

"Oh, I don't know. Something. It will take me time to figure out."

"You know, Kelly, when I was seven, and I was playing checkers with my grandfather, I was completely happy. I never thought I could feel that way again, but I do whenever you're near."

"What are you saying, Kincaid?"

I kneeled down on the front lawn and held up a box of strawberries to her that I had been hiding behind my back.

"Strawberry?" I said. "You look hungry."

"Organic?"

"Of course," I said.

"Better be," she said as she ate one, then two. "They're good. But what's with the kneeling?" Then she saw a black box in the middle of the strawberries, and took it out. She slowly opened the box and her eyes widened. A one-carat diamond engagement ring looked up at her.

"So, Kelly…will you…marriage me?"

That didn't come out right.

"Kincaid—" Her eyes teared up. "How can you afford this?"

"Oh, I don't know."

Old Mr. Leland. I don't know why he lent me the money. Especially considering all the rent I owe. I had to put up with a one-hour lecture on marriage and how he and Mrs. Leland have stayed together so long, though. Listening, he said. I have to listen to Kelly all the time. When I agreed to that, he wrote me the check.

She tried on the ring. It was a little loose.

"The jeweler can fix that," I said.

She gazed at it on her left hand for a moment, speechless, and then took it off, put it in the box, and handed it back to me. She suddenly went rational.

"Well, I have to talk to Mom and Dad first."

"Huh?" I said.

She kissed me on the cheek, and walked back to the car, but all funny, like a girl wearing high heels for the first time. Except she was wearing sneakers. I got up and followed her.

"That's it? That's your answer? Well, how long is this going to take?" I asked.

"You can't just propose to someone you haven't seen for a while. I don't know. I'm going out to visit my parents. I'll be back in two weeks."

"Two weeks? You want me to wait two weeks? Life is in the moment! You have to know now."

She got into the car and just sat there for a while. She was crying a little. I moved closer, and she looked at me. She smiled, then waved good-bye as Cleo pulled out. They drove off slowly. I watched their car drive to the end of the street and turn the corner. I collapsed onto the curb and thought about things for a while. Two weeks. That'll take forever.

I looked the other way, and saw Paul and Vinnie's black sedan sitting a few houses away parked on the street with the motor running. I walked over to it. Paul rolled down his driver's side window and didn't even look at me.

"So?" he said.

"What?" I asked.

"What'd she say?" Paul said.

"How'd you know?" I asked.

"This is Red Bank, kid. We know everything. So—yes or no?"

"She said she's going to let me know in two weeks."

"Let you know? That's no good. Two weeks—that's a little eternity."

I looked in the backseat and saw how disappointed the news made Vinnie, too. I sensed they needed a moment to talk and walked away from the car for a while. Paul then waved me back.

"Vinnie is upset, understandably," Paul said. He took a drag on his cigarette and looked around the neighborhood, then back at me. "The ring—let's have it."

"What?"

"Cough it up," he said. I handed it over. Paul passed it back to Vinnie, who turned on his light and looked at it for a while. He then took out another box, and passed both of them back up to Paul to hand to me.

"Now you're all set," Paul said. I opened the second box, and there was another ring with a huge diamond, maybe four or five carats. I held it up to look at it in the noonday sun. It was brilliantly cut, and much brighter and clearer than the engagement ring.

"I can't take this," I said.

"You'll take it and you'll like it," Paul said. "Plus, you'll need something for the big day. If she says no, we'll take it back. Otherwise, it's yours. Good luck. Now, go make Vinnie and me happy. Go get her." He pulled out and I watched them drive away.

But what do I do next? I mean, waiting two weeks, how am I supposed to do that? I walked around the house and picked up the copy of the *Las Vegas Sun* I got on the trip home. I wondered if there was an obituary for Master Lohan. There was:

Kim Lohan, car salesman in Clark County for the past twenty-four years, eighteen of them at Fingerlake Buick, passed away of natural causes yesterday afternoon at Centennial Hills Hospital. Owner Stan Fingerlake said, "Mr. Lohan was more of a car matchmaker than a car salesman. He would meditate to find the right car for each customer." Mr. Lohan, who won Salesman of the Year awards in eight of the last ten years, was born in Korea in 1945. He left no descendants. Memorial services have not been planned.

I thought of the time we had spent together. Meeting him and shooting off guns. Learning all those poker hands I had never heard of. Catching a shooting Starburst on Tropicana Avenue. Driving cross-country in his gas-guzzling 1970 Buick convertible.

I needed to hear his voice. I picked up my copy of *The Eight Habits of Highly Ineffective People*, and reread my favorite paragraph on page 293, which I had underlined:

Whatever you do, don't become effective at anything. If I see one more "effective" person walking around, I think I'm going to jump out a window. Try to keep failing at as many things as possible, and if you're lucky, you'll make a life of it. Now, that would be a life well lived.

I then remembered a big raking job I had that afternoon over in Shrewsbury. I put the book down and drove over to spend the afternoon raking a three-acre lawn. When I was done, I looked around, saw no one, and ran and jumped into the pile of leaves I had made and looked up into the sky. I watched the clouds float by. I watched the branches conduct the wind. I thought about Kelly and Master Lohan and Edwin and the Lincolns and the bulls in Pamplona.

Sticking up in the leaves next to me, I saw an unused lottery ticket. "Set for Life," it said. I picked it up, and thought about scratching it off. It would be great to pay Mr. Leland for the back rent and the ring, and then maybe even buy a suit, which Kelly said a man my age ought to own. Then I thought, What's the point? I never win at these things anyway, and threw the lottery ticket back into the pile of leaves. Everything's fine the way it is. I then took out both of the rings and looked at them. Staring at the diamonds, I realized that more money would just give me the ability to take another personal-growth course. And that might make me more effective at something, which, the more I thought about it, was the last thing I wanted to be.

But how on earth am I supposed to get through the next two weeks?

CONTACT

If you would like to contact the author or order copies of *The Power of Two Weeks from Now*, you may contact Genteman Press at the address below. Signed copies of the book are available for $25, which includes shipping to anywhere in North America. Bulk discounts are also available. Contact us at:

Genteman Press, Inc.
54 Madison Avenue
Red Bank, NJ 07701 USA

If you would like the author to speak at your gardening convention, bookstore, church group, bowling alley, business meeting, or comedy club, you may contact him at the above address. He has extensive speaking and performing experience, and looks forward to tailoring his presentation to suit the unique needs of your group or event.

Please note that Genteman Press does not accept unsolicited manuscripts.